The Coming of the Unicorn

THE COMING OF THE UNICORN

SCOTTISH FOLK TALES FOR CHILDREN

DUNCAN WILLIAMSON

Edited by Linda Williamson

Floris Books

Kelpies is an imprint of Floris Books
First published in 2012 by Floris Books
© 2012 The Estate of Duncan Williamson

Duncan Williamson has asserted his right under
the Copyright, Designs and Patent Act 1988 to be
identified as the Author of this work

The publisher acknowledges subsidy from
Creative Scotland towards the publication
of this volume

British Library CIP data available
ISBN 978-086315-868-1
Printed in Great Britain
by Bell & Bain Ltd., Glasgow

4323

TO MY WEE EVIE

CONTENTS

INTRODUCTION

This collection of folk and fairy tales has been written down from the storytelling tradition of the Travelling People of Scotland. The author Duncan Williamson was a Traveller who spent a lifetime of seventy years gleaning the lore of Scotland, becoming the country's greatest storyteller of our time (*Guardian*, 22 November 2007).

For over sixty years Duncan Williamson travelled on the roads of Scotland doing jobs here and there in metals, willow, heather crafts and finding employment on farms. He never used a caravan but just built the traditional "bow tent", made of tree saplings and covered with waterproof materials, and travelled on foot, then in the early 1950s with a horse and cart. When the roads got too busy for horses, he sold the horse and bought an old van. And still he travelled on. As he worked his way gradually all round Scotland through Aberdeenshire and Forfarshire, down into Dumfries, all through Inverness-shire, through the West Coast and the Western Isles, Duncan collected all these wonderful stories and tales. The stories are not only traditional tales from the Travelling People, but are also from the crofting people, farmers and shepherds and all kinds of folk.

About his childhood he said:

When I was young we were very, very poor, and I stayed away home in Argyll, near Inveraray. I was born in 1928 in one of these great big tents we call a barrikit – a dome-shaped structure with bow tents on either side. There were sixteen of us; I was the seventh. On a cold winter's night when you had no radio, no television, nothing, and these old paraffin cruisies (open lamps with rush wicks) hanging from the ceiling of the tent, and the fire just on the earthen floor – it was kind of smoky – what could you do with a large family? How could you keep them quiet? You had to tell them stories. My mother could not read, neither could my father. So, they told us these stories that were passed down from tradition which they had learned as children themselves.

So, we were lucky! We had our old grandmother staying with us and she was a great storyteller. She was a wonderful old woman, had travelled far and wide in her young time and collected a lot of tales. We used to do little errands for her and she would tell us stories. My mother's brother Duncan was also a good storyteller. He was a piper, played the bagpipes for pennies and used to travel round the country. He collected many stories. My father told us really old tales. Some were very long, and he would tell us one bit one night and then maybe he'd tell us the next bit the next night, and so on. He wouldn't tell us it all at once! But we had to work for it – we had to get sticks for the fire, get water, run messages and do everything before we got a bit o' our story! This was mostly on the winter nights when it was dark, dark early, and he'd gather us all round about him and tell us a story.

My father worked in a stone quarry with the Duke of Argyll back in the 1930s and he got forty pence a day for breaking stones from six o'clock in the morning till six at night. And there were nine of us going to school at the same time. I went from the age of four till I was thirteen. And we had no school meals, no dinners, nothing. Times were very hard, nothing to spend. I saw me sitting in the school class and I was so hungry I used to say to the teacher, "Please, Miss, can I leave the room?" And she would say, "Yes," and I left and never came back.

I went to the shoreside and kindled a fire and cooked myself some shellfish, mussels and cockles and limpets and whelks to keep myself alive. That was the only source of survival we had. So, we were glad when we came thirteen or fourteen. We left home and took off on our own, left room for the rest of the little ones to grow up. And then we found jobs, used to go to the berry picking and travelled round the country. We would meet up with the rest of the Travelling community, tell stories and collect songs around the campfires.

Oh, the cracks and tales they used to tell round the campfires long ago, you've no idea, hundreds and thousands of them! And there was no such thing as "the children's place" – everybody's place was round the campfire. But they kept it clean and tidy... to attract the children we tellt wir animal stories to keep them entertained till they fell asleep. Everybody had their turn round about the fire telling a crack or telling a tale, telling a wee story or telling something.

"Come on, it's your turn!" Suppose it was only your past experience or something that happened to you in your life – there's so many different types of stories. Travellers never went in for storybook stories, because none of them could hardly read. So, naturally, the stories had to be passed down through the family. There were stories of elves and goblins, and stories o' burkers (body snatchers); there were stories of magic and stories of the devil, stories about wizards and about the Broonie (the spirit of regeneration who often came in the form of a tramp); there were Traveller's stories, stories of all description, homemade stories Travellers made up themselves and stories they heard bits o' and finished off themselves. There were Simple Jack stories, Daft Sandy stories about the village fool, stories about farms and Travellers getting jobs and "near getting burkit" on farms.

Stories about animals were the ones Travellers really liked. Because according to the Travellers in their stories animals can all speak. And some are cleverer and more superior to others. There were holy stories, for the Travellers had their own beliefs, set before the coming of Jesus, and how God created the world. Stories among the Travellers run into countless hundreds; it would take you weeks and months to explain or even tell you some of them.

But all these stories were told not only to weans, you remember! They didn't tell them just for kids. I've seen myself around a campfire in the summertime on an evening, and Traveller men, big men, married men, some grandfathers and old men, and young men as well – all gathered round this fire as interested in somebody telling a story as the day when they were five or six years old! The oldest one maybe seventy, and the youngest one maybe in his thirties, all sitting round a fire telling stories. If children were present the stories came in a line: as the children fell asleep the tales got a wee bit bolder – we'd move from animal tales to witches, or witchcraft attached to the hen-wife – who was very generous and giving and worked the cures. Then came stories about ghosts and haunted grave-yards and haunted wells, and haunted roads. Stories about knights and dragons and enchantment, and water kelpies (sinister creatures who could change their shape), ghost ships, ghost horsemen, warriors and all kinds of things.

With a Traveller who had the name of a good storyteller, as long as he wanted to tell a story, maybe every night for a month, nobody would interrupt him. But when he got fed up and tired, and he wanted to have a smoke and have his tea or go and do something; well, somebody else would tell a story. I've seen men with big lumps o' laddies fourteen and fifteen years of age, young teenagers, drawing their hand across their son's lug and saying, "Be quiet! Don't say a word when the old man's speaking. If you canna listen, go away and play yourself!" These men were interested in stories, big grown men. Why should they no be? Because the stories were really good.

Now you see why stories were so important to the Travelling People. Stories were told to you as a matter of teaching. Because every particular story had its own lesson. Oh, there were many wonderful tales, tales of everything that would teach you to grow up naturally in your own environment in life.

Around Christmas time my father would say, "Well, thank God, this is Christmas Eve. Come doon beside me and I'll tell you a story. Now remember, children, any toy I could buy – what's the sense of buying you a toy when you'll only break it – it'll be destroyed in a couple of days. Even if I had the money to afford it. But, this story will last you the entire time of your life."

My father told me a story when I was only five years old. Now that was seventy years ago! And I can remember that tale the way he told it to me, just the very way. I can visualise him sitting there by the fireside, a young man putting coals in his pipe, you know, smoking his pipe, and all the little kids gathered round the fire; he sitting there telling them a beautiful Christmas tale. Which was far better to us now when I look back than anything he could have bought for us.

Because we were very poor people, we had not only to listen to stories; we had to learn by them. When my father told us his tales, he knew he was going to get through to us. Because after all, it was not maybe telling us how to read and how to write, but my father's knowledge told us how to live in this world as natural human beings – not to be greedy, not to be foolish, not to be daft or selfish – by stories. And by listening, by learning and listening to the old people, you had a better knowledge of the world you had to live in. Stories are something you carry with you, something to last for your entire life to be passed on to your children, and their children for evermore. Telling a child a story implants a seed in their mind, and you know when you are gone from this world that that child is going to tell the tale you told them, and remember you.

When we walked on the roads on the cold winter's day we were wet and tired and hungry, you know, travelling on, each of us carrying a part of our little bundle on our way to help us when we got to a camping place at night. We were miserable and tired. But once the tents were up, the fires were kindling, we had a little to eat, got ourselves dried, then it was story time. The thought of everything else, the day's torture was gone till the next time again. After a good storytelling session everybody was happy. You know, it was great, magical! I've got many wonderful memories of my childhood. Life was really hard. Life was rough and we were very poor. But we were very happy, really happy as children.

I think the happiness comes from the love and respect from parents to children and children for parents. That's the most important thing in all, what really makes life happy for anyone I would say. And that's what our stories were told us for in the first beginning.

* * *

This collection of Duncan Williamson's eighteen Scottish folk and fairy tales for children comprises four previously unpublished stories: "Fox and the Two Cat Fishers", "The Tailor and the Button", "The Kings' Gardens" and "The Cobblestone Maker", and twelve stories originally published by Canongate, Cambridge University Press and Penguin, now out of print. From the early Canongate Scottish Traveller series come "The Miser's Gold", "The Three Presents" and "Jack and the Silver Keys" in *Tell Me a Story for Christmas* (1987); "The Tramp and the Boots", "The Broonie on Cara" and "The Broonie's Farewell" in *The Broonie, Silkies and Fairies* (1985). "The Dog and the Fox", "Jack Goes Back to School", "Johnny McGill and the Frog", "Thomas the Thatcher" and "House of the Seven Boulders" were first published in *The Genie and the Fisherman* (CUP, 1991). "Mary Rushiecoats and the Wee Black Bull" and "The Coming of the Unicorn" were part of the Penguin collection, *A Thorn in the King's Foot* (1987). "The Legend of the White Heather" was Duncan Williamson's first published story, by Oliver and Boyd in *Scotsgate*, 1982.

Linda Williamson

FOX AND THE TWO CAT FISHERS

Now, one time a long time ago on a small farm beside a little river there lived two cats, a black cat and a white one. And the black cat was very old, but the white one was young. They used to curl up in the straw inside the farm building every night. And the old black cat was like me – he was a storyteller. He used to tell the white cat all these stories about himself when he was young, and the white cat got kind of sick listening to him telling all these stories, you know! One night after they had finished their milk by the farm doorway they curled up as usual in the barn to sleep.

The black cat said, "I'm not sleepy tonight, I'd like to tell you a story!"

And the white cat said, "Look, I'm fed up listening to your stories. You've been telling me stories now since I was a small kitten."

The black cat said, "The one I would like to tell you most of all is how I used to catch fish, because I am a great fisherman."

The white cat said, "You catch fish?"

"Of course," the black cat said, "I'm a great fisherman! I've caught many fish in my time."

"Well," the cat says, "we've been hungry many days and you've never tried to catch a fish for me."

"If you come with me tomorrow," said the black cat, "I'll take you down to the little brook and I'll show you how good a fisherman I am."

So the white cat said, "Okay, but let us go to sleep. I'm tired."

And the black cat said, "Tomorrow you're coming with me to the river! I'm going to show you how good a fisherman I really am."

So the next morning off they set the both of them, and they came to the little stream. It was full of little fishes, all swimming up and down by the riverside. And the white cat said, "How do we get these fish out of there?"

The black cat said, "It's quite simple: all you need to do is sit there with your paw in the water, keep your claws out, and hide. When a little fish passes by – just throw it up on the grass."

"That looks quite simple," said the white cat.

"But just watch me," said the black cat, "how quick I can get one!"

So he put his paw in the water and he waited and he waited and he waited. Not one single fish passed by. The white cat went a little bit further up-stream, put his paw in the water, and sure enough along came a little fish. And the white cat went fweesht – out goes the little fish on the grass. The white cat kills it with his paw.

He says, "That's for my supper tonight!"

Now the black cat, he sat and he sat and he sat all day and never caught one fish, till he finally got fed up. He came up from the river and his paw was all wet. It was cold. And there was the white cat sitting with a little fish for his supper.

"You didn't have much luck," said the white cat, "catching your fish, great fisherman!"

"Well, no," he said, "I didn't get one. But I see you have got one."

"Yes," said the white cat, "first time in my life, first fish I've ever caught, and I'm not boasting about it."

The black cat said, "I'm very hungry. Why don't you share it with me?"

"Share it with you?" said the white cat. "My own one little fish

I caught for myself? To share it with you? Indeed I will not; this is coming home for my supper!"

"Please," said the black cat, "I'm an old friend of yours. Why don't you halve it with me?"

So, they sat there arguing about the little fish. Who should come along at that very time but Mister Fox! And he too was hungry. He said, "What's the trouble?"

And the white cat said, "Look, Mister Black Cat here took me down to the river to teach me how to fish. And I caught this little fish. He fished all day and never got any, and he wants half of mine! I am not going to give it to him."

"Well," said the fox, who was hungry and wanted the fish for himself, "that's not the way to treat a friend. You should always halve with a friend."

And the white cat said, "He is not getting half of my fish!"

Now they had sat there until the moon came up and they were still arguing.

"Well," said the fox, "seeing you're being like that, I'll tell you what to do. They tell me that cats are great singers, and they can sing wonderful songs!" The fox said, "You two cats look up at the moon and start to sing and the one who sings the best song will win the fish. I'll be the judge. Do you agree to that?"

Now the old cat, who knew plenty songs because he was very old, thought to himself, I'll win it and I'll have it because I know Gaelic songs and I know plenty folk songs and I've heard plenty old-fashioned songs around the farm. This young cat'll never be able to compete with me.

But the fox said, "Both of you must look up, keep looking at the moon and sing me a song! Then I'll be the judge."

So the two cats, they looked up at the moon and they started to sing, "meow-ow-ow-meow." And they went on and on for about ten minutes. Meantime Mister Fox had gobbled up the little fish! He went on his way.

The two cats sat there till their voices got hoarse trying to sing. And then they stopped. They looked round. Gone was the little fish and gone was Mister Fox! Mister Fox went home to his den and had a good laugh to himself over the trick he had played on the two cats.

The two cats wandered home tired and weary and very hungry. They cuddled up in straw and went to sleep... and that night the old black cat never told any stories!

THE COBBLESTONE MAKER

N ow, boys and girls, I have a lovely story for you. When you walk the streets in big cities there are cobblestones – little stones laid across the streets so that you can walk on them and your feet won't get wet. There's many in the big cities, lots in Edinburgh. And these cobblestones are very hard to make, boys and girls; they are made by little people called cobblestone makers. They work in the great big granite mountains, chip away all day long and make all those beautiful cobblestones.

Now, my story begins a long time ago… for working on a great granite mountain there was a tiny little cobblestone maker. He had a little hammer and a little chisel and would chip away all day long making all those beautiful little cobblestones. And he was so sad. Because whenever he made a little heap of cobblestones someone would come with a horse and cart and take them away, put them on the street. The little cobblestone maker worked all alone.

He said, "Why am I not a very important person? I work so hard to make stones. And someone comes, takes them away and then they walk on my work!" Oh, the poor little cobblestone maker was very, very sad. He said, "I'm just a poor cobblestone maker. No one ever recognises me and no one appreciates my work." And every morning before he would start chipping away at the little cobblestones he would look up at the sky and wish that people would look up at him.

But unknown to him one morning an old wizard was flying home to his home in the mountains and he stopped to rest.

The little cobblestone maker never saw him, but he heard the little cobblestone maker saying to himself, "Oh, I wish people wouldn't walk on my work..."

And then the old wizard said, "Oh, you want to be important do you, little cobblestone maker? *I will make you important,*" and he laughed to himself and flew away. The little cobblestone maker knew nothing of this.

But next morning when he went to his work, before he started he said yet again, "Oh, I wish I was an important person!" And then there was a great flash and the little cobblestone maker was amazed, for he stood there and felt something heavy on his head. He put his hands up to his head and there on his head was a *gold crown.* And he looked at his clothes – he had a red cloak trimmed in ermine – and he said, "I am a king! I am a king! Now people will look up at me, now they will worship me, now they will obey me!"

And he walked through the village. People saw him coming; they bowed and said,'The king has come, the king has come!" and they went down on their knees.

The little cobblestone maker was so happy. He said, "Now I am the king people will look up at me. I am the most important person in the whole world, I am the king!"

Now, it had been a very dull, dull week in the village. The sun had never shone in the village for many days, and as the king walked into the village the sun arose and shone in the village.

And the people of the village said, "The sun has come back. We have never seen the sun for many days," and they turned their back on the king and worshipped the heat of the sun.

The little cobblestone maker said, "A king is not very important; people are turning their backs on me. The sun is more important than me! Oh, I wish I was the sun!" And then there was a big flash... and the little cobblestone maker was high in the sky in the sun. And he looked down at all the people below him as they worshipped the heat of the sun. Now, thought the little cobblestone maker, I am the most important person in the whole world – I am the *sun*. And then, just at that moment a big black cloud came along and blackened out the sun. And the people ran for shelter.

They said, "It's going to be rain. There's going to be a storm, the sun is gone."

And the little cobblestone maker thought to himself, the sun is not important; a big black rain cloud is more important than the sun. Look how the people run for shelter. Oh, I wish I was a rain cloud! And then there was another flash… the little cobblestone maker was a great black *rain cloud* floating across the valley as he watched the people run for shelter. And then, there was a big cloudburst! All the rain fell into the valley and flooded the rivers and carried away the trees and animals, buildings and houses.

And the little cobblestone maker said, "A rain cloud is not important, a rushing torrent is more important than a rain cloud. Oh, I wish I was a rushing torrent!"

And then there was another flash… the little cobblestone maker was a raging *river* running down the valley. He saw the people running to hide and rush for shelter as he carried off trees and buildings. Now, thought the little cobblestone maker, I am the most important thing in the whole world – I am a great rushing river. No one can stop me now! And as he ran down the valley at the foot of the valley there was a great stone cliff. And when the raging river hit the cliff it could not move the cliff, so the river split. One side of the river went to one side and one went to the other side.

And of course the little cobblestone maker who was the raging river said, "A raging torrent is not important. A mighty cliff is more important than a raging torrent. I wish I was a mighty cliff."

And then there was a big flash… the little cobblestone maker was a great, mighty *cliff* sitting at the foot of the valley. Now, thought the little cobblestone maker, everyone will worship me. No one can move me now! I am the most important thing of all. And he stood there, and he stood there. The people admired the great cliff at the foot of the valley. Till one morning.

He felt a little tickling on his back. Tickle, tickle, tickle on his back of the great mountain. And he looked round his back – what do you think he saw? A little cobblestone maker chipping away with his little hammer on his back!

And the great granite cliff said, "A great mountain is not important, a granite cliff is not important; the most important thing of all is a little cobblestone maker. If *he* keeps chipping away on my back some day I will disappear and be gone. Oh, I wish I was a cobblestone maker!"

And then there was another flash, and the little cobblestone maker was *himself* again. Then, he looked back – he saw another little cobblestone maker with his hammer and his little chisel.

And he said, "I won't be lonely any more. I won't wish for anything now – I have a little friend to keep me in company," because there was a second little cobblestone maker chipping away on the hillside.

So, the two little cobblestone makers became great friends. And the little cobblestone maker never complained in the morning. He said, "Now I've got something more important than all the important things in the world – a little friend."

THE DOG AND THE FOX

The old fox had lain in his den all day and he was hungry, because the days before he had been out hunting he had got very little to eat. In fact, he was terrified, because he had been hunted twice by gamekeepers. Nightfall was approaching and he said to himself, "Well, I will have to get something before night, because when it gets dark I'm not going to have much of a chance – all the birds will be roosting and all the rabbits will be in their burrows – I had better go out and get something to eat!"

So away went the old fox. He wandered here, he wandered there, he wandered everywhere that he thought he could find some game for himself to kill. But he could find nothing. He travelled on all his familiar paths, all his old hunting places. But not a hare, not a rabbit, nothing could he find. And the more he wandered the hungrier he got. Evening was approaching fast. So he sat down, considered for a while; he knew that he wasn't going to find anything to eat that night.

He said to himself, "There is only one thing I'll have to do."

He knew it wasn't very far away to the nearest farm because he could see the lights in the distance. But he was kind of afraid to go near the farm in case the farmer was around with his gun – might shoot him for hunting some of his hens.

"If I could only see my old cousin the dog," he said to himself. "He probably has an old bone lying about, or maybe he has not finished his evening meal and would share it with me."

So, he finally made up his mind to go as quietly as he could, go and visit his old friend Cousin Dog at the farm. He knew there was no other way he was going to get anything that night.

Away he went walking up the lane as stealthily as he could so that nobody could see him. Finally, he came to the farm and round to the front where he knew his old cousin Dog had his kennel. By good luck he never encountered the farmer. As he came round the corner to the front of the farm the first person he met was his old cousin Dog! And the farmer was just after bringing the old dog his supper. It was lying in a little dish beside the dog's kennel – there were bones and pieces of meat, all kinds, lying in the dog's dish. The fox saw this and it just made his mouth water!

So, he said, "Hello, Cousin Dog, how are you?"

And the dog said, "Oh, it's yourself, Old Fox!"

"Aye," he said, "it is."

"And what puts you down here at this time of night? I thought you would be away hiding out in your old den up in the cliffs for the night," said Old Dog.

"Well, to tell you the truth," said the fox, "the only reason I've come to visit you – and you know it is not often I come to see you – I'm asking… I just came to ask you a favour."

"Well," said the dog, "we're friends, we're relations. And you never trouble me very often. If there is anything you want and I can help you out, I'll try my best. What is your favour?"

"Well," the fox said, "I have been hungry all day. In fact, I am so hungry I am no able to hunt. The gamekeeper hunted me all day yesterday, never gave me a chance to eat. I am so hungry I can barely walk. I just came down to see you, to see if you had an old bone lying about and any bits of scraps of food you could spare a poor hungry cousin."

"Oh," the dog says, "if that's all that's troubling you, there is plenty here! There's my supper, I've had plenty to eat and I'm no hungry. I'm just about to go for a sleep for the night, and if

I dinna eat it up the farmer will think, what's wrong with him? And he'll no give me any more for breakfast. So, help yourself!"

So, the fox got in to this dish of food, he just guzzled it up as fast as he could. He felt a bit better after he had licked the dish clean. So, he and the dog sat and they talked for a wee while.

"You know," the dog said to him, "Cousin Fox, you are in the wrong kind of life."

"And what makes you think that?" the fox said.

"Well," he said, "look at me here: I sit here and I get plenty to eat, I have a nice warm kennel and plenty straw to sleep in, I get plenty of food, plenty to drink, plenty bones and I have got a great life! You'll have to change your ways."

The fox said, "Ah, certainly! What have you got to do for all this? You must do something. You cannae just stay on the farm all the days of your life and do nothing for all this food and this good bed you get, this nice kennel and everything you do."

"Well," he said, "I guard the farm. And if anybody, any strangers or anybody comes about at night, I bark and waken the farmer up, let him know if there is anybody around about the farm."

"Ahem," the fox says, "well, that is not a very hard job."

"No," the dog said, "the fact is, I enjoy my life and I like it here."

"Well," said the fox, "what would I need to do for to get the same kind of job that you've got?"

"Well," the dog said, "the first thing you have got to do is come on down and see the farmer."

"But if I come and see the farmer," he said, "he probably will shoot me, because I am a fox and farmers don't like foxes!"

"Well, that's true," said the dog. "But the main thing you have got to get first is – you have got to get a kennel."

"Well," the fox said, "I like your kennel. It is fine and warm and comfortable."

"And then," he says, "you get your collar and your chain."

"What did you say?" said the fox.

He says, "You get your collar, a nice leather collar round your neck and a chain."

"And what's the collar and chain for?" says the fox.

"Well," he says, "to tie you up."

"Tie you up?" says the fox.

"Yes," he says, "tie you up!"

"And you mean to say, you stay tied up there all day with a collar and chain round your neck, tied up like a slave?"

"Aye," said the dog, "that's what I do – I'm tied up. Except sometimes when my master lets me out and takes me out for a walk for exercise. But never mind being tied up," said the dog, "life is quite good and your belly is never empty!"

"Ah, no," said the fox, "not me, Old Cousin Dog! I like your food and I like your bed and I like your home. But," he said, "I like my freedom best! So, I will be bidding you goodbye, Old Dog. But thanks very much for the supper. If I ever have the chance to come and see you again, I will return and see you some other time. But you will never get me tied up with a chain or a collar for all the food and all the beds in the world. For freedom is the thing that I love!"

At that the fox was gone, and the dog never saw him any more.

And that is the last of my story.

This is a very old tale and was told to me many years ago by my mother's brother Duncan. He was a great storyteller, old Duncan Townsley. He belonged to Argyll.

JACK AND THE SILVER KEYS

It was in a wee run-down farm in the country that Jack stayed with his mother. It was a good farm at one time but it went to wreck and ruin through the neglect of Jack's father. And Jack was reared up by his mother, and he and her ran the wee bit farm between them. But they ran it mostly down to the ground and things went from bad to worse. They had an old horse and an old cow and a couple of pigs. They were forced to sell them and things got very bad.

Jack said to his mother one day, "If things dinna pick up a bit I doubt I'll have to go and look for a job."

"Son," she said, "it's no a job you're needing; you need to do some work about the place. It wouldn't be in this state if you'd spend more time on it. It's a farm. If you would work harder and plough some of the ground and do some work about it you could make it pay."

But anyway, Jack made up his mind he was going to do a little work on the farm. Looking at a field beside his house that had never been ploughed for years he told his mother, "Mother, probably the best thing I can do is get a loan of a pair of horses and a plough and plough that field, sew a puckle corn or something into it."

So, he got up in the morning, had his wee bit o' breakfast and he went to the neighbouring farm. He asked for a loan of a pair o' horses and a plough. The man was amazed when Jack asked him.

He said, "What are you going to do with it?"

"Well," Jack said, "it came to my mind that me and my mother canna survive much longer if we dinna get something done. Our wee bit o' place is getting run down."

And the farmer said, "That's a good farm. I'll lend you a pair o' horses and a plough if you want to plough that bit ground. Mind, Jack, there are a lot o' stanes into it, it hasn't been ploughed since your father ploughed it years before. In fact, it was once a moor!"

"It'll no matter," Jack said. "I'll be as careful as I can with your plough."

So, Jack got a loan o' the plough and a pair o' horses from the farmer. He took them over. And next morning after breakfast time he went out and he started.

He's ploughing up and down, ploughing up and down and ploughing up and down. And the gulls were following behind him picking the worms up. And he turned some turf with his plough… He wasn't pleased because this part of the furrow wasn't laid down. He went back and tried to push it down with his foot. And he looked in the furrow. He sees this thing sticking up.

He says, "God bless us, what's that?"

And he bent down, picked it up. It was three large keys on a ring. Jack says to himself, "In the name o' God, how did that get there – three large keys?"

Every key was nearly a foot long. Jack looked at them. "God bless us," he said, "they're no made o' iron; iron doesna get that colour. They're no rusty." But he hung them on the shaft of the plough. He ploughed away till about evening and he stopped.

He came in, loosed his horse out and had his wee bit supper. He cracked to his mother, "Oh, Mother, I've a funny thing," he said, "to tell ye: when I was ploughing today that field you tellt me was never ploughed for years, I picked up the queerest thing you've ever seen."

She says, "What was it, Jack?"

He says, "Mother, three big keys on to a ring!"

"No!" she said.

He said, "Aye, Mother, three big keys."

"Jack, Jack," she says, "you dinna ken what you've found!"

"Ha, Mother," he says, "I ken what I found – I found three keys!"

"Aye," she says, "Jack, you found three keys. But you were only a laddie when these keys were lost. You dinna ken the story behind these keys. These keys are made o' silver. Sit down there and I'll tell ye… these keys were the cause o' your father's death and the cause o' this farm getting run down till there's nothing hardly left. It's no worth nothing! Many, many years ago, to be exact, fifteen years ago when you were a bit o' a bairn here, this was a thriving farm. Your father was a good man and a good worker and we had everything we wanted.

"But the king came to visit in the country. In these times there used to be a lot of hunting. There were a lot of wild boars about here. On his rounds, when he stayed near here with the lord o' the district, they went for a boar hunt. And across that wee field belonging to your father the king lost those three silver keys. And the king was never kent to be without these keys, wherever he went these keys hung to his belt. And they went a-missing. Everybody searched high and low. He promised the body that would find the three keys, he'd give them the greatest reward that ever they could ask for. There were hundreds and thousands that searched for them keys and they could never get them. And the king stayed here for nearly a month searching – there were thousands o' folk searching. This place was polluted with folk hunting for them keys! It drove your father beyond endurance. Your father gave up his work, let the farm run in ruin and he spent the entire days of his life searching. Because the king said he'd make any man the richest in the country if they could get him them keys. What they meant to the king nobody knows, but his entire life depended on them. And your father searched night and day. He never did a hand's turn, but out every day searching for these keys. And one night in a night of fog he went a-missing. He never came home and they found his body lying drowned in a ditch. That's what happened to your father. Now, Jack, you've got the king's keys. It's exactly fifteen years ago since these keys were lost. What are you going to do with them?"

"Well, Mother," he said, "what can I do with them?"

"Well," she said, "I hope they bring you better luck as they brought your father. The best thing you could do with them, Jack, is take them back to the king. Take them in, polish them, clean them up. They'll no be hard to clean. And take them back. I suppose the king'll be an older man now, but I think he's still the same king, still alive. And it's a long distance from here, mind ye, to where the king stays in the capital city. But anybody'll tell ye the road and ye canna go wrong. I'm telling ye for your ain good: keep them hidden and dinna tell naebody ye have them but the king!"

"Well, Mother," he said, "they're no my property. And I'm no worried about the reward."

"Oh, Jack," she said, "ye'll be highly rewarded if you can get to the king with them. But if you ever breathe a word about the keys, ye'll never see the king alive – because you'll be robbed and murdered and they'll be taken from you. Forget about everything, Jack. Never mind, I'll get the laddie from the neighbouring farm to finish that wee bit ploughing and sow a wee puckle corn to keep the wee cow going. But the best thing you can do is tomorrow morning pack up your wee bit o' gear, take a wee bit with ye and set sail. Get them keys back to the king. I suppose you'll get the reward. And I'm telling you, it'll be no wee reward at that! But will you do me one favour?"

"Well, Mother," he said, "you're my mother… what would you want me to do?"

"That was the cause o' your father's ruin," she says, "and I would like to ken what they're for and what do they open?"

"Well, Mother, if I can find out what the keys are for and what they open, and if I'm able to get back … I'll try my best and find out for ye!"

"Okay then," she said, "that's a promise!"

So, the next morning, true to his word Jack got up early, had his wee bit breakfast, made a wee parcel o' meat to himself, whatever he had about the house, put the best bits o' clothes he had on him and said goodbye to his mother. He set sail on the road. And he walked, he walked and walked. He asked folk this and he asked folk that, but he kept the keys hidden in the lining of his jacket. He wouldn't show them to a soul.

But he must have been on the road for three or four weeks and his clothes began to get tattered and torn. He got kind o' rough, he never shaved, barely took time to wash his face. His boots began to get worn down. But he finally made his way to the capital city where the king's palace was. Now, he didn't go straightaway forward up to the palace demanding an interview with the king. He wandered about the town two or three times asking this and asking that, finding all he could find out. But finally he found out that the king was home and his queen was home, and Jack made his way to the king's palace. The first body he met at the palace was a guard.

And the guard stopped him, "Where do you think you're going? Where do you think *you're* going to?"

"Well," Jack says, "I want to see the king."

So the guard looked at him. "You," he said, "want to see the king? What do you want to see the king for?"

"I've got a wee message for him," Jack said. "I want to speak to him."

He says, "You tell me and I'll tell the king."

"No," says Jack, "I'm no telling you what I've got to tell the king." And it rose a heated argument with them.

But just by good luck on Jack, who came walking up behind

the guard's back but the king himself, an aged man, about sixty years of age!

"What's going on here," he said, "guard?"

"Your Majesty, it's this rough looking character of a man here who wants an interview with you, the king."

"Well," the king looked at Jack. "He seems a fine specimen o' a man to me, suppose he's a bit rough. He's probably a traveller on the road. He's one of my subjects I suppose." The king said, "Where do you come from, young man?"

"To tell the truth," Jack said, "Our Majesty," and he bowed to the king, "I came a long way from here." Jack told him he came from such-and-such a place, "And I came to see ye. In fact, I brought a present for ye."

"Well," said the king, and the king smiled. "You brought a present for me? This is very good o' you. Come with me!"

The guard wasn't very well pleased. As Jack walked past the guard he looked daggers at Jack, you know, Jack with his rough coat!

The king walked into his chamber with Jack and he told Jack to sit down. The king sat down.

"Well, my young man," he said, "would you care for a drink?"

"To tell you the truth," Jack said, "Our Majesty, drink is a thing I could never afford. I've never had very much time for it."

"Anyway," he said, "you'll have a glass of wine with me before you tell me your story." And the king was very pleasant. So, he called for two beautiful glasses of wine and he and Jack drank the wine together. "Now," he said, "young man, what have you got for me? What have you come to see me about?"

Jack rammed his hand down into his coat in below his oxter. From a big long pocket he pulled out the three keys. He held them in front of the king.

And the king looked. The king's eyes came out in his head. And the king started to shake; the excitement got the better of him. For a minute he couldn't speak.

"Young man," he said, "do ye know what you've got there?"

"To tell ye the truth, Our Majesty," he said, "to me they're three keys."

He said, "Where did you get these keys?"

"Well," he said, "you, when I was only an infant, were hunting a boar across my father's land, a wee farm.

"I remember it well," said the king.

He said, "You came for a visit to your country to see some o' your landowners. I believe ye lost these keys." And he told the king his name was Jack.

"Well, Jack, you don't know what you've done for me."

Jack said, "I never did anything for you, Our Majesty; they're your property and my mother advised me—"

"By the way, how is your mother?" the king said. "I remember a long time ago stopping by her little farm to water the horses and she was a pleasant woman."

Jack said, "My father died searching for your keys."

"Oh, bad luck," said the king, "very bad."

"He searched," Jack said, "his entire life for to get your keys. One night in a fog and mist he was lost, he ended up drowned in a ditch."

"Oh, I'm very sad," says the king, "very sad to hear about that. And you, my young man, how did you come by these keys?"

Jack says, "Me and my mother had a wee bit argument about the farm getting run down. But I didn't know anything about the keys. She never tellt me. Probably if she had have told me about the keys I would have ended up the same as my father searching for them."

"Ha!" the king smiled, "you'll probably be after the reward too."

"Well," said Jack, "it would come in handy!"

"Oh, but," he said, "don't worry, my young man, you'll be highly rewarded."

"But, Our Majesty, will ye do one thing for me? Will you tell me what these keys are for?"

"Well, Jack, I'll tell ye. I'll tell ye part o' the story, but I can only tell ye the first half; I canna tell ye the second. I had a great friend here belonging to me many, many years ago that lived in the court with me. He was a wise old man. He was a court magician. And he and I used to be the greatest o' friends. But he had to go away back to his own land, he never mentioned where. And before he left he gave me three silver keys: and these three keys open three gates to a special garden. I used to go and visit that garden whenever I felt the mood taking me. And I lost the keys! Thereafter I could never enter through the gates of that garden."

"Well, Our Majesty," Jack said, "I'm very happy you can go back to your garden."

"Jack, you've no idea what you've done for me. Ye've made me a new man!"

"Oh," he said, "I did?"

"I want you to be highly rewarded! You can have the whole privilege o' the palace. You can have everything you want. But you must make me a promise that you shall not leave for twenty days – till I come back. I'm going on a visit. But I want you to have everything that you require under the sun. Don't spare anything!" And he called for the head cook and he called for the head footman. He called for the head o' the guards and he warned them all, and called for the queen, and tellt them, "Jack must have the run o' the palace – see that he wants for nothing! But," he says to Jack, "have another drink!" So, he and Jack sat and they had another drink. They cracked away about good things. He was a very pleasant man, the king.

"Now, Jack," he says, "a footman will show ye to your room. And I want you to stay there. Make me a promise that you'll not leave the palace or the district for twenty days till I come home!"

So, the king bade goodbye to Jack and he said, "I'll no be seeing ye in the morning, but remember I'll see ye as soon as I come back!"

So, Jack went down to the dining hall and he had a good time to himself. He had plenty to eat, plenty to drink. He had a nice clean-up, a right bath and a nice change o' clothes. He really enjoyed himself. And the footman showed him to a lovely bed. He lay down on this beautiful silken bed and relaxed. But he hadn't been in bed for more than an hour when he heard a knock on the door.

Jack got up, "Who's there?" he said.

"Oh, it's me the queen. I want to talk to you," she said very sternly.

Jack opened the door, came out, bowed to Her Majesty. "Your Majesty, what can I do for you?"

"It's no what you can do for me," she said, "it's what *I'm* going to do for *you*!"

"Your Majesty," he said, "I have everything I need."

"Oh," she said, "you've everything you need, have you? Well, you're going to get more than you need," and she came in, shut the door behind her. She said, "You know what you've done?"

"Well," Jack said, "I've done nothing. I've nothing to be ashamed of..." Jack thought maybe he had talked rough to some o' the lassies when he had a wee drink with some o' the maids in the palace or something. And he tried to think back in his mind what he had done as a mistake, but he couldn't think on anything he had really done, what he had done to annoy the queen. But he racked his brains and racked his mind – "I must have done something," he said to himself, "to annoy the queen."

But the queen was standing; she's terrible wicked and wild. There was no reasoning with her.

And he went down on his knees, "Your Majesty," he said to the queen, "what have I done that makes you so upset?

"You!" she said. "I was happy and happy married to the king... You have come and destroyed my life!"

"Oh," Jack said, "Your Majesty, I never destroyed your life. I never did any harm. All I did is come here and give the king back his keys."

"That's what you've done, destroyed my life by giving the king back his keys!"

"Well, I didn't know about this." But there was no reasoning with the queen. The more she talked the angrier she got. So, Jack begged upon her to tell him what was the reason behind the keys.

Within her anger she says, "One night, when the king was drunk he told me the story."

Jack began to cock up his lugs; he wanted to find out.

She said, "His good friend the wizard, before he left, built a secret garden in the mountains, in the middle of the mountains and guarded it by three gates, so that nothing in the world could ever enter – unless they were to be opened by the three silver keys. And in that garden is a fountain. That fountain is the Fountain of Youth. Whoever spends a day there in that fountain loses a year o' their life. And for every day that he spends he gets younger by a year. So now," she said, "I was happy with the king, growing old with the king. What's going to happen to me now when the king comes back a young man and me an old woman? What will he do? He'll cast me aside like a bit o' stick and take some young woman for his queen. *You* are the cause o' that!" And she got angrier and angrier. She called for the guards: "Arrest that man! He insulted me!"

Immediately the guards came and Jack was arrested, thrown in the dungeons. He was taken before the court the next morning and the penalty for insulting the queen was death. Jack was to be hanged, hung by the neck until he was dead for insulting the queen! There was no escape for him. And he lay in a wee puckle straw, the rats running over the top o' him days out and days in, fed on as little as possible and barely a drink o' water. Till Jack says to himself, "I wish to God I had never seen the silver keys."

But anyway, the days passed by and Jack lost count of time. He barely knew day from night from a wee bit light shining through a slit in the wall in the dungeon. His beard grew long and his coat got tattered and worse he got. Till one day the door was flung open and in marched three guards. They pulled Jack to his feet.

"Come on, get on your feet, you insulter of the Royalty! Today you're going to be hung."

So, Jack was marched out by the courtroom to the square. The scaffold was built in the square and the people were all around, hundreds of them to see him hung. They were shouting and flinging stones at him as he was pulled by the guards. The guards were trying at the same time to hold the people back... that anybody, a stranger, would come into their district and insult Her Majesty the Queen! It was a great disgrace. It could never be lived down. But Jack was stood up, marched up the thirteen steps to the scaffold and the rope put round his neck. He was to be hung!

The hangman says, "Your last request before you get hung!"

Jack said, "I've no request to make. But if this is the way that ye treat a poor innocent man," he said, "who came into your country with a present and greetings for the king... and I never insulted the queen!" But he pleaded and probed with the man, but it was no use with the hangman.

He was just ready to pull the trap to let Jack hang – when down through the crowd o' folk came this horseman! And a voice rang up, "The king, the king! Make way for the king!"

And this man rode up. He came right beside the scaffold, jumped off his horse, ran up the thirteen steps and took his sword, cut the rope around Jack's neck and led him down the steps.

And Jack looked. He looked again. "Thank God," he says, "somebody's saved me!"

"Jack, Jack," he said, "what happened to ye?"

And Jack looked… the voice was familiar but Jack didn't know who the man was. And he was dressed like nobody Jack had ever seen dressed before in his life!

He says, "Jack, do you no ken me?"

"No," says Jack, "I dinna ken you!"

And the people all went down on their knees. "Back, go back," he said to them, "make way for the king!" He says, "Jack, come with me, I want to speak to ye!"

Jack was glad to be saved. He said to himself, "I'm no caring who he is, but definitely he saved my life. He's a king to me!" Jack was mesmerised. He didn't know who this was – but this young man lifted him, rode him up through the crowd o' folk. The folk left an opening and let them pass by. The man took him right up, up to the palace, to the king's palace. In they went into the great chambers.

And the man called for two glasses o' wine. He handed one to Jack. Jack was that shaken with fright he could hardly drink it.

"Calm yourself, Jack," he said, "you're safe now. Nothing's going to bother ye. Ye're home and I'm home."

Jack was still amazed. He didn't know what was wrong. This young man, well, in his forties, never the same man that… Jack didn't know who he was!

He says, "Jack, do you no ken me? I'm your king!"

"Ha!" said Jack, "well, you're no the same king that left here afore I went into that dungeon."

"Aye," he said, "Jack, I'm the same king."

"Oh, aye!" said Jack. "Well, will ye do me one thing: will ye tell me about it? I'm lost and I'm in a terrible state – I was near hung! I was charged–'

"I know what you're charged with," said the king. "That's why

I rescued you. But don't fear, don't fret. Don't worry. Everything is going to be all right. But sit down and calm yourself. Take a good glass o' wine and we'll talk it over. You tell me your story first, Jack, the truth! And I'll tell you mine."

"Well," Jack says, "after I bade good night to ye, I enjoyed myself and I went to the ballroom. I had a few drinks and I had a good feast. I had a good wash and good clean-up and I went to bed. And the queen came in. And she accused me of coming here with a present for you, the keys. She tellt me the story that you would ride to the Garden o' Youth and stay there for twenty days, and come back twenty year younger. And then you would have no more time for her. I tried to reason with her but was no use. And she said I insulted her, called the guards and I was arrested and thrown in the dungeons. And I must have lay in the dungeons for twenty days."

"Oh," he said, "you look in a terrible state, but never mind, Jack! For the twenty days you spent in the dungeon she'll spend the same." He said, "Send for the queen immediately!"

And the queen was sent for. The queen came in. He told the queen, "Sit down there. You know what you've done? Now own up! What did Jack do to ye?"

She says… she couldn't tell a lie to the king.

"Now," he said, "don't tell me any lies. I don't want to hear any lies! I want the truth!"

"I knew," she said, "that Jack brought back the keys to you, and you would go…" and she started to greet. "You would go to the Garden o' Youth and you would come back a young man. You would have no more time for me. You would probably take a young queen and I'd be cast aside. I accused him, he was the cause o' it. I was happy as I was."

And he said, "You, for that, would get a young man hung while I was gone – in my absence? Woman, you ought to be ashamed o' yourself! You, my queen that spent your entire life with me, think

41

that I would do a thing like that on you! My full intentions, after I had had my spell in the Garden o' Youth, was to send *you* to the Garden o' Youth for your spell. You're still my queen and you're still my wife. I love you. But if you think that anybody else could take your place with me, then you're not fit to be my queen! I'm not going to forgive ye; you are going to the dungeons for the same length o' time that Jack spent in the dungeons, for twenty days. And by that time you'd better think over it... you're going to suffer the way that poor Jack suffered, the man that gave me eternal life!" he says to the guards, "Take her away!"

Away go the guards with the queen. She's put in the dungeons.

The king ordered for Jack to get everything he required under the sun, and he and Jack sat down and had a good drink. He said, "Jack, I must apologise for the queen."

And Jack says, "Well, I was nearly hung, and it's an awful thing to be nearly hung."

"Oh," said the king "it's a bad thing to experience. I believe it! But let her suffer – she'll be all right."

"No," said Jack, "no. My poor old mother is back home and she'll be worried about me. I couldn't go back to my mother and tell her that the queen spent twenty days in a dungeon, even suppose... I'm a man and I could take it. But no, our queen couldn't spend twenty days in a dungeon!"

He said, "Jack, is that the truth? Are you ready to forgive the queen for nearly getting you your death?"

Jack said, "Aye."

And the king rose, he clapped Jack on the back. "Jack," he said, "look, you're a better man than me ..." He sent his guards. "But I'll tell ye something," he said, "she's going to apologise to you when she comes back!"

So, they sent for the queen and the queen was brought out in front of the king and in front of Jack.

And the king turned round. He said to the queen, he smiled

and laughed, "You, as the queen, my queen, sent this young man nearly to his death. And now *he's* going to pardon *you*. *I* was going to put you for twenty days to the dungeon, but *he* wouldn't allow it. And he is the greatest friend that ever I have had," and the queen started to greet. He said, "Jack has forgiven ye. And tomorrow I'm taking you for a journey to the Garden o' Youth."

And the queen was so excited that both the king and Jack had forgiven her that she started to cry again. So, she called for one o' her maids.

Jack turned round to the king and he said, "Our Majesty, I think it's time that I was going to see my old mother."

"Well," said the king, "we'll be going in the morning anyway. But remember, Jack, you're no going without your reward!"

And the queen said to one o' her maids, "Go into my bedchamber and bring me one o' the finest diamond necklaces that I possess. And give it to Jack to take back to his mother in token of my gratitude for saving me from twenty days in the dungeon!"

And the king went ben and came out with two bags of gold. He places them down on the front of the table and says to Jack, "Now, Jack, that's for you. That's your reward. And go to my stables. Get the finest horse that you can find. And the finest suit o' clothes and anything else you want under the sun – just take it for the asking." And the queen and king bade Jack goodbye. But he says, "Remember, Jack, if you ever come my way, don't be feart to stop in, because you're my greatest friend."

Jack says, "If you keep carrying on and getting younger the way ye do, I'll probably no recognise ye!"

"You'll recognise me, Jack," he said, "because if you don't visit me, I'll come and visit you! And you never ken, maybe some day *you* might take a wee trip to the Garden o' Youth!"

The next morning Jack packed up, took his two bags o' gold and his diamond necklace, got a fine horse and rode back to his mother.

And when he sat down, he told his mother the same story as I'm telling you. He bought a great big farm with all his gold and he became a big farmer. And he could still be around to this day because I heard late in the story, that Jack and the king paid a visit to the Garden o' Youth!

And that's the last o' my story.

THE THREE PRESENTS

Many years ago there lived an old woodcutter and his wife in the forest. He made his livelihood mostly by collecting and selling wind-blown sticks, stuff that was blown down by the wind. In these days saws weren't very popular and he couldn't afford good wood-cutting tools. He just used whatever he had. So, he and his wife managed to struggle away and make a kind of living with the little bits of wood he could pick up in the forest, as he got them free.

But coming round by the wintertime it came a very heavy storm of snow, and it was deep in the forest. It just took him bare than busy to get as much that would keep his own fire going, never mind to sell to keep him and his wife going. So, three days he tried his best to get a few sticks for sale; but no success. The snow was far too deep.

So, he comes home and he says to his wife, "You know, I've tried my best and things is in a bad situation. The snow is too deep. I don't know what's going to come of us."

"Well, John," she says, "you'll have to try your best and do something, because the winter's coming on hard."

"I know. But," he says, "what can I do? Have we nothing we could sell?"

"No, nothing we could sell."

"And," he says, "we can't borrow anything from anybody because we've tried and we owe a lot of money to a lot of people."

"Well, John," she says, "you'll have to swallow your pride and do one thing: you'll have to go and see your three rich uncles, ask them for some money."

Now, John didn't like this idea. But anyway, for his wife's sake he made up his mind he would swallow his pride and go and see his three rich uncles that he had never seen for many's a year. He had a long way to go.

So, early next morning his wife makes him a wee bit lunch in a bag and away he goes. He travels for two days till he comes to these rich uncles who are three rich merchants, three brothers. He comes to their door.

Oh, they made him that welcome! Poor John… they always felt sorry for him, wondered how he was getting on. So, he stayed with them and they asked him how was his wife, and oh, they gave him everything he could ask for. He never mentioned how financially he was off.

So the next morning he says, "Before I go I'd better bid you farewell."

One brother says to the other, "Poor John, we'll have to give him a present."

"What shall we give him?" says one.

"Money," says the other. "I think we should give him some money. It'd be the best thing for him. We'll give him some money to help him on his way, he's so poor."

So, between the three of them they managed to raise up a hundred silver shillings. And they put it in a bag and they gave it to John. Now before he left they told him, "John, when you go back to the house, don't be extravagant and give it to your wife and let her spend it all at once. Try and make it do you for a while till you're able to get more work."

"Right, uncles," he said, "I'll do that." So, he bade them farewell.

Away he goes with his hundred silver shillings and he plans and talks it over to himself on the road home, he'll hide it when he gets back to the house. When he landed home he searched the house for a hiding place.

In one corner of the wee house where he stayed his wife had a heap of rags, old rags. He takes his wee bag of silver shillings and hides it under the rags. Every wet day the wife was needing a couple of shillings, he would go and give a few to her, never telling her or making her any wiser how much he had or where it came from.

But one day the snow disappeared. And who came to the door but a ragman collecting, asking the lady if she had any old rags lying around for sale – he would give her a shilling or two.

"Yes," she said, "I've a heap of rags in the corner." So, she gathered all the big heap of rags in the corner, John's bag with his hundred shillings and everything, gave them to the ragman.

The ragman thanked her very much and away he goes.

That evening John came back from the forest. First thing, he went to see that his silver shillings were there… but the lot was gone.

"What have you done, wife, with all that heap of rags that was in the corner of the house?"

"Oh, John," she said, "there was a ragman here the day and he gave me a sixpence – I gave him the whole lot."

"Oh, dear-dear-dear," he says, "my beautiful bag of money!"

"What money?" she says.

He says, "I got a hundred silver shillings from my uncles and I hid them among the rags!"

Oh, the wife was heartbroken, you know.

So, for the next two-three days and a week things got as bad as ever. They were stuck again, nothing doing. John couldn't get any sale for his sticks. So, the wife coaxed him the best way in the world and made him once again promise he would go to see his three rich uncles once more.

Back he goes to see his rich uncles. Oh, they make him welcome, poor John! They bring him in, give him the best they had to eat, keep him for the night, talk to him all night, give him a good drink, everything he requires. They asked him how he got on.

And he turned round and told them what happened.

They said, "We told you…"

"But," he said, "I hid the money in among the rags and my wife gave the rags away to the ragman!"

"Well, John," they said, "we'll have to do something for you again." So, they searched their pockets between them, and all the money they had was fifty silver shillings. They gave him fifty silver shillings.

"Now, John," one says, "remember – hide it where your wife won't find it!" They bid him farewell.

True to his word, John goes away back. This time he hides it in a dustbin at the side of the house, the old dustbin. He works away a couple of days, gives his wife a shilling now and a shilling again. Till one day the dustcart came, a man with his horse and cart collecting the ashes. In these days they called at the houses and asked if you had any ashes to lift, and you paid them a penny or two for taking away your ashes and dust.

"Oh, yes," she said, "my dustbin's never been emptied for months! Will you empty it for us, please?"

So, the dustman came and emptied the ashes into the dustcart and away he goes.

When John comes back from the forest the first thing he goes to look in his ashbin… it was empty.

"Wife, wife, wife! What have you done?"

She says, "What?"

He says, "Who emptied the ashbin?"

She said, "The ash cart was here today, the man with his pony and ash cart was here. I gave him the old ashbin to empty."

He said, "My silver shillings were in the bin – fifty silver shillings I got from my uncles."

"Well," she said, "they're gone."

"Oh, wife, wife," he said. And the wife felt very sad, you know, about this. She couldn't speak. She was just nearly in tears. But anyway, John forgave her.

He said, "We'll just try our best. But don't ask me to go back to my uncles any more for any more money because I'm not going, in no way!"

"Well, never mind, John," she says, "we'll have to try. You'll just have to work all the harder and see will we manage to keep ourselves alive. But I'm really sorry."

"Oh, well, wife, it canna be helped. It was only a mistake."

But anyway, time passed by and they managed to survive the best they could. Till one day a carriage pulled up at the door. Who was it but the three rich uncles who had come to pay John a visit!

John's wife met them at the door, welcomed them in. She said, "We have nothing to give you to eat. Come in, we've nothing to give you to drink. We're very poor."

"Oh, where's John?"

"John will be home in a minute."

John came home. "I'm sorry, uncles," he says.

"But," one says, "I thought we gave you a hundred and fifty shillings – that should have kept you through the winter."

John says, "I hid it as you told me – in the dustbin. And my wife gave the dustbin away to the ash cart, and also therein was my fifty silver shillings."

So, the two uncles were furious. They rose to their feet.

"John," one says, "you are a foolish man. You don't deserve any money. We were foolish ever to give you money in the first place."

The other says, "You can't look after any money, John. You're better without it. No wonder you're poor!"

"But, wait a minute," says the third uncle. "I've something in the carriage that's good enough for him to look after." And out he goes to the carriage and fetches in a lump o' lead, a square lump o' lead. He crashes it down on the table.

"There, John," he says. "A lump o' lead is all you're fit for! When you can't look after money maybe you can look after a lump o' lead." And away they go, jump in the carriage and bid John farewell.

So, the wife took the lump o' lead and she placed it on the windowsill. Days passed by. They forgot all about it. But one day, it was a beautiful day, they heard a knock at the door. This is a fisherman.

"I wonder," he says, "I forgot my matches. Could you give me a light for my pipe?"

"Sure," says John, "come in and have a cup of tea." John fetches him into the house, gives him a cup of tea and gives him a light for his pipe.

And he's sitting looking around him. He sees this lump o' lead lying on the windowsill. He says, "Is that a lump o' lead you have there?"

"Yes," says John, "it's a lump o' lead. It's all I'm fit for to look after! It'll lie there…"

"Wait!" says the fisherman, "would you give me that lead? For a long time I have been searching for a lump of lead just like that to hold down my nets, my fishing nets."

"I'll take it," says the fisherman, but I'll make you one promise – that I'll bring you the first and finest fish that ever I catch when I put that lead on my net!"

"Oh, well," says John, "please yourself!"

So, away goes the fisherman. But true to his word, the next day up comes the fisherman. And he has this most beautiful fish you ever saw – a great big cod! And he comes into the house, lays it down.

"There," he says, "that's for you and your wife. It'll make a lovely supper for you. That's the first fish that was in my net when you gave me the lead – the very thing I was needing." And he thanked him very much and away he goes.

"Well," says John to his wife, "that was very nice o' him. At least the lead got us something, something worthwhile at last."

True enough, says the wife, "It's a good fish… I've never had a bit o' fish for years."

"Well," he said, "the sooner you get it cooked the better!"

She took the fish into the kitchen and split the fish up. And when she split up the fish's stomach out popped this ring! With a red ruby stone it was just the most beautiful ring you ever saw in all your life. And she cried to John, would he come and see this!

And John took it. It was just the most beautiful ring, a rich blood-red ruby. And John's heart was just fair taken with this ring. He put it on his finger and he said he would never part with it.

But they hardly sat down for a minute at the table to enjoy their fish when they heard a knock at the door. This was a rich merchant passing by. He said he was on the way to sell his wares, would they give him something to eat till he and his caravan got to the town?

John says, "We're very poor and humble people, but come in and share what we've got. We're only having fish."

"Oh," says the rich merchant, "fish is the very thing I need." And he told all his train of people to wait for him while he went in and enjoyed a bit with John and his wife. He looked at John, and he said to him, "That is a lovely ring you're wearing."

"Ah, yes," said John, "it's a beautiful ring."

He said, "Will you sell it?"

"Oh, no," John says, "it's far too beautiful to sell. It's far too beautiful!"

"Oh," says the rich merchant, "it's something like that I've been looking for, for many's a year. I would really give you a lot of money for that ring."

"Well," says John, "how much would you really give me for it?"

He said, "I'll give you a thousand silver shillings for your ring."

"Done," says John, "you can have it!

And the rich merchant paid John a thousand silver shillings for his ring. John and his wife had plenty money to keep them going for the rest of their days.

And that's the end of my story.

THE MISER'S GOLD

A long time ago in a small village there lived a poor widow-woman who had only one child. She used to find bits of jobs in the village to help keep her and the child alive, but things began to get very bad with her. Work was finally running out. She tried to take up sewing and washing and everything else to help her and the baby survive, but it was no good. There was no more work for her. This is when my story really starts – on Christmas Eve.

The mother raiked round the house for something to make a bite for the wee child but it was no use. She could find nothing. And she was very sad about this. She sat down and started to weep.

The wee child was about three years old and she spoke to her mother, "Mommy, why are you crying?"

"Well," she said, "I am crying because I have nothing to give you and this is Christmas Eve. All the children in the village are preparing for their great Christmas parties, and their mommies and daddies have been down the village and bought all these wonderful presents. Why is it on Christmas Eve that you and I have to be so poor that I haven't even a single bite to give you, never mind a present?" And she started to cry again.

Then, she thought and wondered what she would do. She said to herself, "Probably if I go down the street I might meet some of my friends and I could maybe borrow or beg something off them."

But as it was a cold winter's day she didn't want to take the wee child with her. So, she called the child to her, "You wait, dearie, by the fire there, and mommy will go down the street and see if she can find some of her friends she used to know. Perhaps they will give me something or I can borrow some money from them and I will get you a present for Christmas – when Christmas Morning comes in I will have a present for you!"

So, the wee child sat by the fire and the mother wandered away down the village. Every place she went everyone was sitting behind their locked doors and their lighted windows preparing for Christmas Morning. Christmas trees, Christmas lights up, everything was so nice. And she walked the streets for nearly two hours but could find not one single soul she knew.

Now, by this time the wee child got fed up waiting for her mommy to come back, and the fire burnt low, nearly out. The house was beginning to get dark. She got up… and she was such a beautiful wee child she was, with gold, hair, a head of golden curls. She walked out the door and down the street to look for her mommy. There was snow on the ground and she didn't know where she was going… Eventually she was lost. But, she saw this light up a path leading up to this house. One light in the window. She walked up and right into the house to the fire. The fire was burning bright. The room was bare, bare as could be – one table, one chair. On the floor at the front of the fire was a sheepskin rug. The wee girl sat down and heated her hands. She sat and then started to cry for her mommy. But no one ever heard her, no one bothered. And she lay down on the sheepskin rug and fell asleep.

Now, unknown to this wee child, this was the house of the village miser. He was the most miserable and miserly man in the whole village, who seized every penny, would give nobody nothing and would hardly buy a bite for himself. He was away out walking the streets to see if someone would invite him in for Christmas and give him something – before he would spend a penny – and he had thousands in gold! But he wandered among the snow till he got fed up. He couldn't get anybody to give him anything, him being a miser. Everybody was in behind their doors on Christmas Eve.

"I will go back to my own house" he said to himself, "and I will have a nice heat by my fire. I will go to my bed and I will not spend any money for Christmas."

So, he wandered back and when he landed at his own house he walked in through the door. The first thing he saw was the fire burning down low. The reflection of the light was shining on the baby's golden curls lying on the sheepskin mat on his floor.

And the miser said, "Someone has been at my money! Someone has been at my gold, scattered and stole some of my gold!"

And he ran forward to pick up the gold. He got down on his knees and he put his hands… he felt the child's hair – he looked down and he saw the child sleeping. He lifted her up in his lap. And she was still asleep. She put her two arms round his neck because she thought he was her mommy. He let her sleep and went to put some sticks on the fire, then got up on the chair and took the child in his arms. He sat there for nearly an hour with the child in his arms.

"I wonder where you come from, little one," he said. And then it dawned on him. He had seen the widow woman further up the street a bit with this baby, but it was younger then.

By this time the child's mother had come home. When she found her house empty, the fire out and the child gone she was in a terrible state. She didn't know what to do. She had got nothing, met no friends, nobody. She was heartbroken and to find her child away made it worse. Just then, she heard footsteps – there was a knock on the door.

She said, "Probably that's someone who has found my child," and she ran out to the door. Here was the miser with the child in his arms! He walked in. Oh, she was so happy to see the miser. She knew who he was but she had never spoken to him.

He said, "I found your child asleep on my mat by my fire."

"Yes," the widow said, "she must have wandered away to look for me. I was down the street looking to see if I could find some of my friends who would help me out because I have nothing to give her to eat, no money to buy her a present."

And then the miser felt so sad he could hardly part with the baby he had in his arms, but he handed her over to the widow. He said, "Look, you sit down there until I come back. I will find a present for the baby."

The miser runs back to his house, flings the door open, never even takes time to close the door, walks up to his hidden place where he has all his gold, pulls out the box. There were gold coins in their hundreds! He fills his two pockets with coins and walks down the street. He goes to the first big store he can find – luckily it is just before the store starts to close for the night. He walks in. The man behind the door of the store was amazed to see the miser coming in. A change had taken over the miser altogether, a complete change. Gone was the miserable look all through his face, his eyes were shining brightly.

And the man behind the counter said, "Something queer has come over the miser. I've never seen him look like this before."

And the miser started to buy. He bought and he bought and he bought. And the man behind the counter was wondering how he was going to pay for this – him being the village miser. Everybody knew how miserable he was! But he bought, as much stuff as he could, and he could barely carry everything he needed under the sun for the widow and her child. And he filled this great big box, he carried it up on his back, took it into the widow's home.

"Now," he said, "put on a big fire!" And she put on a big fire, and he placed the box on the table.

"Now," he said, "go and make something for us to eat!" And the widow was so delighted she could have kissed him, she could have fair kissed the miser! And he had this big poke of candy. He took the wee child on his knee and gave her candy. And the widow went away to make supper. She had as much foodstuffs that would have done her for months! She made a good supper for her and the miser, and they sat and they talked. They talked and they talked, and the child fell asleep.

So, they put her to bed and the miser opened another box. He took a great big Christmas stocking and he hung it aside the fire, packed it full of Christmas toys and stuff, and the widow was so delighted. She started to cry.

He said to her, "Everything will be all right. Everything will be all right!"

She said, "I have no friends, I have nobody. And I was so down and out until you came."

"Well, you have a friend here now," he said. "People in the village would give you nothing, and the people down the village would give me nothing because I was the miser. You were a poor widow. But tomorrow morning it's Christmas. We will spend it together and have the best Christmas that any of the two of us have ever had."

And so they did. They had the greatest Christmas they ever had in their lives. Shortly after that the miser married the widow and they never wanted again for anything else for the rest of their days.

And that is the end of my wee story.

JACK GOES BACK TO SCHOOL

After many years Jack had grown very old. He had a family. His wife had died, and he came to live with his youngest daughter in a little cottage by the roadside. She had five or six little children. And these children loved their grandfather old Jack very, very much. They sat in his lap and he told them stories, he told them about how he'd spent his entire life, how he'd met his wife and how he had travelled all over the world, how he'd met goblins and elves. And every night was a different story! These children were enthralled with old Jack, with Grandad's stories. He put them to sleep every night in bed. And his daughter Mary, she loved her father. Her husband said, "Look we dinna need to worry as long as he's with the children." And sometimes the children fell asleep in his lap by listening to his stories.

But in these bygone days there were no cars on the road. It was all horses and carriages. But where he lived Jack's son-in-law, Mary's husband, was a woodcutter. And he went out to cut wood every day. And old Jack he said to himself, while his son-in-law was at work and the children were in school, he would work in the garden. He would tidy up the garden and grow vegetables. He was more than eighty years old, and he was still Jack!

But one day he was working in the garden when, lo and behold, he saw a coach, four horses and a coach, passing by. And he saw something falling from the coach. The horses drove on. He stepped out o' the garden and he walked out to the road. It was a rough old road in these bygone days. And lo and behold there was a handbag, a permanty they called it in these days, a carrying bag. It's lying in the road! Jack picked it up; it was heavy. He opened it up. It was full, full of money. He carried it back. He took it in. His daughter was busy working in the kitchen. He went up to his bedroom and he hid it under his bed. Jack rubbed his hands together.

He said, "I've got golden sovereigns for evermore! Nobody's going to get them from me… I'm still Jack!"

Now, he had a plot in his head. He said to himself, "Look, I know where it's come from. This is the tax collection – people collecting the taxes around the town and the country. And it fell off the coach. But," he said, "it's mine." Now, Jack being Jack, he wanted to know how in the world he could come to keep this money. So, being Jack, he got an idea in his head. All day he sat in his room and he thought about it. And then the children came back from school that day.

The laddies and lassies, they all gathered round grandfather as usual and they said, "Grandad, tell us a story, tell us a story!"

He said, "I'll tell you a story." He told them stories past the common till they fell asleep.

But the next morning at breakfast time he said to his daughter, "Mary, my lassie, I'm going back to school."

She says, "Dad, you canna go back to school!"

He says, "I'm going back to school – this morning I go! Give me a pair o' scissors."

She says, "What are you wanting scissors for, Dad?"

He says, "To clip my trousers short."

She says, "Dad, have you gone crazy?"

"No," he said, "I'm no going crazy. Give me a pair of scissors!" He got a pair o' scissors and he clipped his trousers above his knee. He said, "Weans! Come here a minute, have you any old schoolbags lying about?"

"Aye, Grandad," they said, "we have. There's two-three schoolbags there."

He says, "Have you any books lying about you're no wanting?"

"Aye, Grandad," they said.

Mary said, "Where are you going?"

He said, "I'm going with the weans to school."

"Oh, no, Grandad," they said, "you canna go!"

"I'm going with you to school today," he says. He cut the trousers short, put them on his legs. He got a bag from the weans, he got two books, he put the bag on his back and he went with the weans. They walked to school, and he sat in the classroom with the weans in school.

The teacher said, "What are you doing here, Jack?"

"Aye," he said, "I'm back to school. I want to learn to read, same as the weans, learn to read."

But anyway, he sat in the school all day with his short trousers on, with his schoolbag and his books. And he sat with the weans for one day in the school.

But he walked back with the weans that night and he told them stories. He did everything, put his bag away. And the next morning he was out in the garden as usual. The weans were off to school. He never went back to school any more. Only one day he had gone to school.

But sure and behold, he's in the garden close to the road when what should come driving up but another coach! Two men and their long hats and batons hanging down by their pockets. They pulled in. They stopped the coach by the side of the road.

They came and said, "Old man, you're busy?"

"Well," Jack said, "I'm busy."

"Well," one said, "you know who we are: we're the justices, justices o' the peace."

"Oh," he said, "I see, I can see by your coats and your tails and your batons – you're justices of the peace."

"The problem is, old man," they said, "the problem is we want to talk to you. The coach passed here two days ago. And we have lost a permanty with a lot of money. It fell off the coach. Have you by any chance seen it?"

"Oh," Jack said, "that's true. I saw it!"

"Oh, you did?" they said. "Oh," the one looked to the other, "ye've seen it?"

Jack said, "Aye."

He said, "Have you any idea where it is?"

"Well," he said, "I saw it, eh, let me see now... The four horses and coach passed by. It fell off and I picked it up, I carried it up and I put it alow my bed."

"That's good enough," said the two men, "we have the right person. We've got him, right! Do you still have it?"

"Oh," he said, "I still have it."

"But," one says, "when did this happen?"

"Well," he says, "wait a minute now... It was the day afore I went to school."

He said, "Old man, what do you mean?"

Jack said, *"The day afore I went to school!"*

He said, "How old are you, old man?"

"Well," he said, "I'll be eighty-six on my birthday. Come my birthday I'll be eighty-six!"

And they said, "When did you pick up the bag with the money?"

"Well," he says, "the day before I went to school I picked up the bag!"

And one justice says to the other, "Look, come on, let's stop wasting wir time with a silly old fool!" And they drove on.

And Jack was left with the bag of money. He shared it with his wee daughter and they lived happy ever after.

MARY RUSHIECOATS AND THE WEE BLACK BULL

Little Mary's father and mother were out going to the village with a pony and trap when there came a terrible storm. The pony got frightened in the thunder. It ran away, bolted, and little Mary's father and mother were killed in the accident. She was left all alone – no one to take care of her. Then, after her mother and father's services had finished, they were buried. Lo and behold, one old woman came forward.

And she says, "I am Mary's grandmother and I want to take care of the child."

So, everyone was happy. People in the village thought that poor Mary didn't have any friends or anyone to take care of her, but up turned the old grandmother. Little Mary went to live with her and this is where my story begins.

After a spell of time and many tears, Mary had cried because she missed her mother and father very much, she finally settled down with her grandmother in a little cottage beside a large forest. Her grandmother was a nice and kindly old soul and she loved Mary dearly. She kept some hens, some ducks and mostly geese, a lot of geese. Granny used to every month go to the market and sell some of the male geese, which she had brought and reared up, and kept the female geese to produce more. So, Mary really came to love her grandmother after she forgot about her daddy and mommy. She stayed with her grandmother for many, many months. Now she began to feel she was at home at last. She'd found someone who really did love her. But, her grandmother was very poor even though she owned some geese and some ducks and hens; because the few pennies she got at the market she used to buy food for herself and for little Mary. But one evening Grandmother was sitting knitting by the fireside.

Mary came in by the fire and sat beside her, said, "Granny, you know it's all right for you to sit knitting here, but it's not very fun for me."

And then Granny said, "Why, Mary, why?"

"Well," she says, "I don't have any friends to speak to. I can't play with the hens or the geese or ducks that you have and I feel very lonely."

"But, Mary, you have me!"

"But, Granny, some days you're knitting and some days you're ironing. Some days you're working and I need someone to speak to, someone to love and someone to take care of."

"Well," she says, "Mary, probably I might get you a dog or a cat."

"No, Granny, I don't like dogs and I don't like cats."

"Well, then, Mary, would ye like to come with your granny to the market tomorrow?" The old woman felt very sad for her wee granddaughter. It was her only son's daughter and she wanted to do everything in the world to please her and make her feel at home.

"Oh, yes, Grandmother," she says, "I would love to go with you to the market tomorrow."

"Well," she said, "Mary, if you want to go with me, you must go to bed bright and early and make sure that you're up to help me tomorrow, because I've got seven geese and we're going to walk them to the market. We'll sell them, get some money and then everything will be okay, and you'll see some people there."

"Oh, Granny, I would love to go..." Because she had never been with her granny to the market before.

Now, in this market all people came from around the country and they sold their animals. Some sold sheep and some sold goats; some sold calves and some hens, and some sold ducks. And they all met in the market in the village once a month. Mary's grandmother used to always make sure that she took something to sell at market. And when she sold something, it kept her going in money till she had something else to sell. But Mary never knew much about this. This was a new experience to Mary.

So, she was so excited that night when she went to bed she could barely sleep. Her grandmother had promised that she would buy her something in the market that would make her happy. True to her word, next morning Mary got down from her bed and she walked down. Granny was up. They had little to eat – they were very poor – some goat's milk and some porridge.

And Grandmother said, "Now, Mary, you promised you would help me."

And Mary said, "Yes, Grandmother…"

So she and her granny gathered seven of the fattest geese they could find in the yard. Granny took a stick and Mary took a stick and both of them drove the geese, walked them to the market. Mary was running in front and keeping them out of gates. Granny was coming behind and driving the geese. They hadn't far to go, maybe about two miles. When they landed in the market, the man they heard who was auctioneer knew Mary's grandmother very well. He saw the fat geese coming in. He helped and put them in a pen. Once the geese were penned in the market, they would be sold as seven fat geese. Grandmother took Mary and she bought her a wee bit o' lunch.

"Now," she said, "Mary, we'll come and see the things getting sold."

There were goats, sheep; there were cows, bulls, calves, all getting sold in the dozen; hens and ducks and geese. When you have something to sell you must wait your turn. So, the auctioneer sat up there and he sold cattle, sheep and ponies, goats and donkeys, everything till it came to Mary's grandmother's geese. And he sold them. He sold everything that was in the market; but lo and behold, one thing he didn't sell was a wee black bull calf, a wee calf – nobody seemed to want it.

Everybody was finished. They bought everything they needed. They went their way. And lo and behold, the wee bull calf was left on its own in a pen. And Mary after walking round and seeing all the animals, she came up beside the wee bull calf.

She put her arms round its neck and said, "I love you, you're so nice," and she petted the wee bull calf, a wee black calf.

Grandmother was up by the auctioneer getting paid for her geese. She came down and searched for Mary. She couldn't find her. And she went round the ring, all the pens searching. Then she found Mary sitting beside the wee calf with her arms round its neck.

She says, "Come on, Mary, it's time to go home. I've sold my geese and everything that's in the market's closing down for the night. We must go home."

"But, Granny," she said, "how about the wee calf here? It's never been sold – there's no one to take care of it."

"Mary," she says, "I don't know who owns it."

"Granny," she said, "please, Granny, buy it for me!"

Granny says, "What in the world would you do, Mary?"

She says, "It'll be company to me. I'll take it home with me and I can look after it. I can talk to it and I can feed it grass. It's a pet I want; I don't want a dog, not a cat, Granny. Buy me this wee calf, please!"

"Well," says Grandmother, "I have got some money for my geese today. I'll go and see the auctioneer and see what he says about it."

So, old Granny, to keep Mary happy, walked up to the auctioneer and said, "You've sold everything in the market today?"

And the auctioneer said, "Yes, everything apart from one wee calf, a bull calf. Nobody seems to want it."

"Well," she said, "would you sell it to me?"

And the auctioneer knew the old grandmother. He says, "Granny what will you do with a bull calf? It will grow into a bull; it will probably get you into trouble when it grows up to be a big bull. It'll no be a calf for long."

She said, "Would you sell it to me? My wee granddaughter has made friends with it and she wants it. She won't have anything else. I've offered her a dog or a cat, and she has not time for hens or geese."

"Well," the auctioneer said, "it's not worth very much. It's only just a wee black calf. I don't know where it came from. It came in among some cattle today. Some farmer brought it from the forest and said it wasn't his. Nobody seems to own it. Nobody seems to know who owns it… Why, if you want it, I'll not sell it to ye; I'll give it to ye because the market's closing. Take it with you if you feel fit!"

"Thank you!" says the old granny. "You sure you don't want some money for it?"

"No," says the auctioneer, "I don't want any money for it, because there's not an animal left except it in the market – take it with you if it's any good to you. But bring it back when it gets big and I'll sell it for you!"

The old grandmother toddled down. She was very old. She toddled down to Mary. Mary was sitting with her arms round the wee calf and it was licking her hand. It was just a wee black calf about seven or eight weeks old and its eyes were shining as bright as stars. Mary had her arms round its neck.

Her grandmother says to her, "Mary, we have to go home."

"Granny, we can't go home. Not tonight we can't go home and leave this little creature itself, because it has no one to take care of it."

She says, "Mary, *you* can take care of it!"

"Oh, Grandmother, did you get it for me? Did you buy it for me?"

"Yes," she says, "Mary, it's yours. From now on it's yours. You have it, you keep it and I hope it'll be good to you. Take care of it, because it's your friend and I got it for you."

Lo and behold, they opened the gate. Mary and her old grandmother walked out and the wee black bull calf followed them. It followed Mary as if it had known her for many, many months. So, Grandmother got a few messages on her way that she needed to buy. They walked home to their little house near the forest and the calf walked with them, behind them. And Mary just loved it from the heart – every step she was taking she was looking back to see was it still there – but it walked on behind her, its nose behind her all the way!

She says, "Grandmother, I love this like nothing else. I don't want dogs, I don't want cats. I want nothing!"

Now, Mary wasn't very old, she was about twelve, a handsome young lassie with long hair, beautiful young girl. So, they walked home to their little house beside the forest as Mary was so excited. There was nothing in the world that meant anything to her but this calf.

"Granny," she said, "we'll find some place for it to sleep?"

"Oh, Mary, you'll find it some place to sleep. We'll put it in one of the sheds that's empty now. The geese are gone. We'll put it in the shed that the geese used to be in."

So, no way in the world… before Mary got a bit to eat that night, she took it into one of the sheds where the geese slept. She made a bed for it of beautiful hay. She brought it a pail of water and she put it – she never tied it – she put it in the shed. And after she had taken care of it, she walked in to her grandmother.

They had a little lunch together and her grandmother called her beside her. "Mary, come here and I want to talk to ye. Sit on my knee, Mary," and Mary sat on her grandmother's knee. "Now," she said, "you must understand, ye're growing to be a big girl and you've got something to take care of."

"Oh, Granny, I love it so dearly. I love my calf so dearly. Granny, I'll look after it. It'll not be any trouble to you in any way. I'll look after it. I'll take care of it, feed it and it'll not give ye any trouble. But please, please, Granny, please, would you give me a promise?"

And Granny says, "Yes, I'll give you a promise."

"Granny, please will ye never sell it?"

"Oh, well, Mary, if you love it so much as that, I'll not sell it."

But anyway, they began to settle down and times passed, months passed by. Mary took care of her calf and Granny took care of the hens and her ducks. And Mary loved her calf. She went walking with it. She took it everywhere she went. But Mary walking with her calf and feeding it and taking care of it, her clothes began to get kind o' withered, tattery and torn. One day she came in.

Granny says, "Where have you been, Mary?"

"Oh, I was out in the forest walking with my calf."

"Mary," she says, "ye're in a terrible state. Your coat is torn and it's ragged. Ye know I'm very poor and I canna buy ye a coat or anything."

"Granny," she says, "well, patch it for me!"

"No, there's too many patches on it already. I can't put another patch in it."

"Well, Granny," she says, "make me a coat, knit me a coat!"

"Mary, I canna knit ye a coat. I don't have enough thread. But I'll tell ye what to do, Mary; my old grandmother a long time ago was very clever and she taught me many things. If you will go out into the moor, in the rushie moor, and cut me some rushes, I'll make ye a coat."

"Oh, Granny, ye couldn't make me a coat from rushes!"

She says, "Mary, I'll make ye a coat like the old people used to do a long time ago. If you make up your mind to cut me some rushes like the rushes I want, I'll make ye a coat!"

Well, Mary was very pleased. "Granny, I can cut ye rushes." And beside where they stayed was a rushie moor where all the rushes grew very high, five foot high. And people long ago used to split the rushes up. They wove them; they could make cloth from them like they do with the flax. So, Mary made up her mind that she was going to have a coat. She went into the back of the shed. She got an old sickle that was used by her grandfather who had died many years before, and she went on the moor. She cut the rushes, bunches and bunches and bunches of rushes. And the calf came with her.

The calf was nodding, pushing her with his head and he's nodding with her. He played and he jumped and he cocked his tail round his back. He ran round the field. Mary was still cutting the rushes. The calf was always with her, but it was getting bigger and bigger as the days went by. Mary gathered bundle and bundle and bundle o' rushes. She brought them back. And her granny sat. She split them down, took the hearts off and she weaved them. She sat and weaved them day after day, day after day. And lo and behold, she made Mary a coat – the most beautiful green coat that you've ever seen in your life. Nobody in the village had a coat like this, because it was made from rushes.

When Granny was finished with the coat she said, "There you are, Mary, there's your coat!" And Mary tried it on. Mary loved this coat like nothing in the world. She put it on and it just fitted her, made from rushes.

So, she used to walk to the village; Granny smoked a pipe and she used to go for tobacco and some things for her. And when all the people in the village saw Mary coming, they saw her with this strange coat on made from rushes. Even the children used to call her "Mary Rushiecoats". But Mary visited the village many,

many times and the people in the shops said, "Oh, here comes Mary Rushiecoats again with her wee black bull."

Wherever she went the black bull-calf went with her. And the calf got bigger and bigger as the days went on.

Now, many months had passed by. A year had passed by, two years had passed. And Mary Rushiecoats still had her coat and Mary Rushiecoats still had her black bull-calf. Mary and her calf enjoyed life together like nobody in the world did. And Granny still sent her to the village and the bull went with her. Now, the bull-calf was getting so big that sometimes when Mary got tired, she used to jump on the bull's back and the bull would walk with her on his back. No bridle, no saddle, nothing. This was Mary's pet from the world. And the people in the village always said when she came, "Here comes Mary Rushiecoats and her black bull." Everyone knew Mary Rushiecoats.

But life with old Granny became very hard, because she had no money and her hens didn't lay. Her ducks didn't lay and the geese didn't lay. Things began to get worse and worse for old Granny. And she wanted to take care of Mary… It came market day once more. One night Granny called her, "Mary, I want to talk to ye."

"What is it, Granny? What's the trouble?" Now, by this time Mary had grown into a beautiful young woman and the bull had grown into a beautiful young bull.

She says, "Mary, tomorrow's market day and I have very little to sell. My geese have not grown. I have no hens to sell. I've nothing. And, Mary, I'm very sad to say this to you, but we need money very badly."

"Well, Grandmother," she says, "what can I do?"

"Mary, I'm sorry, to ask you. But I was wondering if we could sell the bull in the market and get some money for me and you?"

"Oh, no, Granny, Granny, Granny!" she says. "No way in the world. Suppose we starve to death, Granny, I cannae sell my bull."

She said, "Mary, look, he's getting too big now and I canna see that we need him any more. You've had him for—"

"I've had him now, Granny, for two years and he's my pet and my love. I love him and we have great times together – Granny, I could never part with him in my life!"

"But, Mary, I'm your grandmother and I'm getting old. I cannae supply food and clothes for ye any more. I had to make you a coat from rushes and we need the money. Wouldn't it be nice if we sold the bull and we got some money, because someone will take—"

Mary says, "Someone will take him! They'll kill him and use him for food. They'll kill him. No way I'm going to sell my bull!"

And Grandmother said, "Look, Mary, tomorrow we must sell the bull, there's no other way!"

Mary was very upset at this. She just walked upstairs and went to bed, never even said goodnight to her grandmother. Went to bed, but she couldn't sleep. No way in this world, no way could she sleep. Her grandmother went to bed. And she waited and she waited till she thought her grandmother was asleep. Then, lo and behold, the moon came out, the moon was shining clearly. Mary quietly slipped down the stairs, as quietly as a mouse, and walked out to the shed where she kept the bull. She put her arms round the bull's neck and it rubbed its head against her.

She said, "Little friend, Granny wants to sell you for money. But I'll never sell you, no way, little bull. I'll never sell you." And the bull rubbed his head against her. She says, "Me and you, we're going to run away – where they will never find us – we'll go into the forest. I'll take care of you and you can take care of me. We'll run away into the forest!"

So, the moon was shining and Grandmother was asleep. Mary quietly opened the shed and then she walked away. The bull went with her. Off they went into the forest and they travelled and they travelled, and they travelled for many, many hours.

When old Grandmother wakened up in the morning she called for Mary. Mary was gone. She walked down and she called round the place, round the shed. But Mary was gone. And she walked into the little goose shed where Mary kept the bull. The bull was gone. Grandmother was upset and she wondered what happened, but Mary and the bull were gone. But the old grandmother worried. She went back in, she made herself a cup of tea and she was upset. She searched. She called and shouted and she tried her best to find them. She looked round all the fields and all the moors, thought they were out for a walk or something. But no way; Mary and the bull were gone. So, now we'll leave old Grandmother for a little while and we'll travel with Mary and the bull.

But as usual, when people travel, Mary got tired and Mary got hungry. She was so hungry and so tired. She came to a large tree at the end of the forest. She put her back to the tree and she sat down so exhausted she couldn't go another step. So hungry, so tired, so exhausted after travelling so many, many miles she couldn't go another step!

When the bull came up, it put its head right beside Mary and it spoke to her. It said, "Mary."

Mary just… she said, "You can speak to me?"

And the bull said, "Yes, Mary, I can speak to you. I didn't want to speak to you before but I want to speak to you now. You have run away with me. You have saved my life. Your grandmother got me. You took care of me and now it's up to me to take care of you! What would, what is it that you would like?"

"Oh," Mary says, "little bull, if you really can talk to me and do any wonderful thing… I'm hungry and I'm tired. I'm hungry – I need something to eat!"

"Look in my ear!" says the bull. And Mary looked in the ear and there in the bull's ear was a wee bit o' cloth.

"Pull it out!" said the bull. And Mary pulled the wee bit o'cloth out.

"Put it on the ground!" says the bull. And Mary put it on the ground. Lo and behold, when the cloth was spread on the ground, there was the most beautiful things in the world to eat that Mary could ask for. There were sweetmeats, there was food, there was everything that Mary could ask for – fruit, vegetables, meat, everything. And the bull just stood there with his head nodding.

And Mary said, "Is this for me?"

And the bull said, "Eat to your heart's content, Mary." It shook its head there, it never said another word.

So, Mary sat and she ate and she ate. She ate fruit and vegetables, she ate meat till she was so full she couldn't go another bite. She wondered to herself, why is this happening to me? Is this my bull?

And the bull said, "Are you finished, Mary?"

And she says, "Yes, I've had a lovely session. I've had everything I need to eat."

"Well," he said, "throw the crumbs on the ground and put the cloth back in my ear!" And Mary threw the crumbs on the ground. She finished and put the cloth back in the ear.

"Now," says the bull, "put your arm round my neck and we'll go on wir way!"

So, Mary put her arm round the bull's neck and they walked on and they walked on, for hours and hours, till at last they came to the end of the forest. There was no more forest. There was an open plain and grass growing as high as the bull's feet. Mary and the bull made their way through it. When lo and behold, they came to a cliff-face, a great cliff, and there was no passage. They couldn't get by no way in the world.

And Mary said, "We can't walk through the rocks. We've got to go this way."

And the bull says, "No, Mary, we'll go *this* way. Follow me!" And Mary followed the bull. He said, "If you're feart, hold on to my tail." And they came to a narrow passage in the rocks. Mary gripped the bull's tail. And the bull went on and on and Mary's holding on to his tail when they pass through a narrow passage. Lo and behold when they came to the end of the passage there was a great valley. And the bull stopped.

Mary said to the bull, "Why are you stopping?"

And the bull turned round. He says to Mary, "Look, Mary Rushiecoats, you must remember; Mary, listen to what I tell you and do what I say. Have no fear! But if anything ever happens, don't have fear, just listen to me and do what I tell you!"

Mary walked up. She put her hand round the bull's neck and they walked forward. But they hadn't walked more than two yards when, lo and behold, right before them was the greatest, biggest, ugliest looking ogre they ever saw in their life. He's standing there right before them!

And he said, "Where are you going? Why have you come here? Why have you entered my valley? No one is allowed into my place!"

Mary was terrified and the bull whispered quietly to her, "Fear not, Mary, have no fear!"

And the ugly ogre-hunchback said, "O-oh, such a beautiful calf! It'll just make such a wonderful supper for me."

And he came over and said, "Come with me, both of you. Because I've been at hunting today and I have not found any deer or anything. But now I found a wonderful calf that'll give me such a wonderful supper. Come with me!"

And he caught the young bull by the ear and he pulled it. Mary hung on to the bull's neck. He pulled it by the ear and led it in through the valley up to a great castle built among heavy rocks. He pulled the bull by the ear.

And the bull went naturally. It never did anything, just went –

pulled by the ear by this great ogre who was big and ugly. He half pulled the bull, half forced it, and poor Mary is hanging on. She's wondering what's going to happen. But she doesn't know, and she believed what the bull had told her, have no fear! Then, up they came to this large castle in the cliff, wonderful castle built on the rocks. And the ugly, big hunchback pulled them into a large room. On the floor were a great big fire and a great pot boiling. The ugly ogre pulled and he shoved them in this room.

He turned round to Mary. "Now," he said, "you, woman, you must make me something to eat. Because I've been hunting today and I'm starved from hunger. I need something to eat! I've got myself one fat calf that needs to be roasted and boiled and made me for something to eat! But I'm tired and I'm hungry. And woman," he said, "if you don't make me something to eat, you shall die!"

Poor Mary! She was upset. She was trembling in her shoes. But she knew that the bull had told her to be calm. The bull-calf never said a word. And poor Mary Rushiecoats stood there.

Then the great ogre said, "There is my bed and there is my fire! There is my pot and there is a knife on the table. And I am tired and weary. I am going to sleep. You'll kill that calf and put it in the pot and make me something to eat."

The great ogre stretched out in his bed. He was the ugliest ogre you ever saw – hump on his back and plooks on his face and long fingernails and curled toes. But he owned all this great castle. And he's lying in bed because he was tired. And Mary and the poor bull-calf are standing there in the great hall with a great fire burning, the great pots by the fireside.

When lo and behold the bull spoke to Mary, "Mary, don't be afraid, little one. He'll be asleep for five minutes and ten minutes and fifteen minutes. But now and again his voice will speak to you. But listen: when his voice speaks to you, it won't be talking to you; it will be talking to *me* – but we'll be gone! Take the knife on the table and cut my ear!"

"Oh," Mary says, "no way can I cut your ear."

"Please," said the calf, "cut my ear. Cut my ear, go on, Mary! Cut behind my ear!"

"Why," says Mary, "should I cut your ear?"

He says, "Cut my ear and get three drops of blood from my ear!"

So, Mary took the knife, shaking and trembling and worried, and wondering what she'd do with her wee calf.

He says, "Cut my ear, Mary, don't be afraid. It won't hurt me in any way. And take three drops of blood from my ear. Put them beside the fire, and then me and you shall escape."

So, Mary took the knife and she cut the calf's ear, behind his ear. And she took three drops of blood. She put them – one drop there, one drop there – on her chair by the fireside.

The calf said, "Mary, search round the kitchen and see if you can find some salt, a wee bit o' salt."

And Mary ran around the kitchen. And lo and behold, there was a bag o' salt. She took a handful o' salt and the calf said, "Get two handfuls o' salt and find a wee bag. Put it in the bag!" So, she took two handfuls o' salt, put it in the bag and he says, "Mary hang on to that and don't let it go – for the peril of your life – don't let it go!" said the calf.

Mary did what the bull-calf told her, because whatever the calf had told her seemed to work out all the way and she believed in it.

"Now," said the calf, "climb on my back!" And Mary climbed on the calf's back. "Put your arms round my neck, Mary, and we shall be gone!"

So, Mary put her arms around its neck. And the calf went out through the door and was gone. It went perump, pitterohn, pitterohn, pitterohn, running and running, running as fast as he could go.

"Hold on, hold on, Mary," he said. "And it doesn't matter whatever happens, don't let go of my neck!"

So, wee Mary Rushiecoats didn't know what to do. She's holding on to the bull-calf's neck and the calf's running on and running on to try to get away from the ugly monster.

But back in the castle the wicked ogre has wakened up, and he called for food. "Is it ready, yet, woman, or I'll eat you alive? I'll eat you the way you are!"

And the first drop of blood from the calf's ear said, "Not yet!"

The ogre stretched back. He fell back. Then he lay again, lay for a few minutes. And Mary and the calf's running on and running on. And the ogre said, "Is it not ready yet? I'm getting hungry – I'm dying for something to eat – have ye roasted that calf for me yet, woman?"

And the second spot o' blood said, "Not yet, it's not ready yet, but will soon be."

And the ogre lay back once more. And then, Mary and this bull-calf ran on and ran on and ran on once more.

When lo and behold the ogre wakened up once again and he said, "Woman, it must be ready now!"

And the third spot o' blood said, "Yes, it's ready. Come and get it!"

And the ogre got up. He rubbed his eyes and he walked to the pot – it's empty. And he saw – "They have deceived me," he said, "they have deceived me! There's nothing in the pot," and he put his hands in the pot – nothing! "Where is my calf and where is that woman?"

And with his vision he looked out and he saw them in the distance: the black calf and Mary Rushiecoats on its back – they're running on and running on. "Oh," he says, "they may run, but I'll get them before the night is out!" And the ogre set off as fast as he could. He's running as fast as he could.

Mary and the wee black bull, they're going and going and

going. They're running fast, when they came to a lake. There was no more land, only a lake. And the bull said to Mary, "Hold on, Mary, hold on. Don't be afraid. Hold on to my neck!" And Mary held on to his neck.

And the bull – into the water – he swam and he swam and he swam. And Mary looked back. She saw this evil ogre coming. He's coming paddling as fast as he could be. He's fw-wooph, fwi-i-iphf sucking the water as he's coming. As fast as he sucks, the faster they go. The more he sucks the closer they're getting to him.

And the bull said, "Mary, throw in the salt, throw in the salt!"

And Mary took the bag o' salt. She couped it in the water. And lo and behold, the minute she put the salt in the water, there came an iceberg of salt. A mountain, a mountain o' salt.

And the ogre came and he's whoooo-opf sucking, and he's spitting and he's whooochk sucking and he's spitting all the salt out. Because he couldn't take the salt! And he ran, and he ran, he's sucking the salt and he's spitting the salt. By the time he spits the salt, Mary and the bull are getting farther and farther away. And he's spitting the salt and he's sucking the salt – trying to get after them.

Then lo and behold they came to the end of the water. Mary and the black bull came to the land once more. And when they came to the land it was a long narrow valley, cliffs and high sides, as high as the cliffs could be.

But, after he spat out the water the ogre still made his way. The evil ogre made his way as fast as he could after them. After he spat all the salt from his mouth he managed to scramble out of the lake. And he's crawled on his hands and knees.

He spat the last mouthful out, said, "I'll get them before the day is out!" And he came through the valley.

The bull says to Mary, "Hang on, Mary, hang on. It's not much further now!" They rode through this narrow cliff, high precipice on each side, narrow cliff for as far as the eye could see.

And then the ogre's coming as fast as he could, hurrying as fast as he could.

He said, "I'll get them before the night is out!"

They reached the middle of the valley, this high-cliff valley, and Mary said to the bull, "We're not going to make it. The ogre's going to get us!"

"Don't worry, Mary," said the bull. He turned round and he said, "Don't worry, Mary. Look in my ear, my other ear, and see what you see!"

And Mary looked in his ear. She picked out a pea, a wee green pea.

He says, "Throw it behind you, throw it behind you, Mary!" And Mary took the wee green pea. She threw it behind – in the passage that they went through – and there, when the pea hit the land there was a magnificent explosion. The whole valley seemed to explode in fire and flame. The rocks came tumbling down behind them. And the bull stopped.

And he said, "Now, Mary, this is it. You don't need to worry any more. This is it!"

"Tell me," said Mary, "tell me, little bull, what's going on?"

"Mary," he said, "don't worry. We must turn and go back."

"Go back?" she said. "No way am I going to go back!"

"We'll go back now, Mary," he said. "Get off my back and lead me back!"

Mary got off his back. And when she led him back, there was the ogre buried to the neck in boulders and rocks. Only his head showing, his ugly head. And Mary and the bull walked up. The bull stopped beside the ogre.

He said, "Look, Ogre, this is the final end for you. Ye know what ye've done to me!"

And the ogre said, "Please, please, set me free, set me free!"

And the bull said, "You set me free first – *before* I set you free – you set me free!"

And the ogre said, "All right, I'll set you free if you set *me* free."

"No!" said the bull. "I'll not – till you set me free – *you set me free first*," said the bull.

And the ogre spoke some words from his mouth.

Lo and behold, after the ogre spoke these words, there was a great change… The bull was gone for evermore. And there stood the most young, handsome man you ever saw in your life! He stood there before Mary. Mary was upset! She didn't know what to say. The most handsome young man in the world you ever saw stood there dressed in green and a sword by his side.

"Now," said the ogre, "I've set you free – set me free!"

"I'll set you free," said the young man, and he took his sword. He whipped the head off the ogre! The ogre's head fell over and rolled down in among the rocks.

Mary hid her eyes. She says, "What's happened?"

And the young man put his arms round Mary. He says, "Look, Mary, little Mary Rushiecoats, it's a story I have to tell you: I was the apprentice to that ogre and he had magical powers. You see, he reared me up and taught me all these wonderful things. But all these things were evil – I didn't want any more. And I tried to escape. He turned me into a calf and sent me to the market to get slaughtered, so that I could never indulge in his powers and tell anyone. But you, Mary, have saved me from disaster."

He put his arms round Mary and he said, "Mary, the ogre's castle is mine because it was mine before. It'll be mine again – and you must come with me and be my wife for evermore!"

"But," she says, "what about poor Grandmother?"

"Don't worry about Grandmother, Mary," he said. "We'll find her, and we'll bring her here with us. She'll live here happy ever after." And so they did.

And that is the end o' my story.

THE TRAMP AND
THE BOOTS

N ow there are many wonderful things you can learn about the fairies, and things connected with fairy stories. According to the Travelling folk's idea, all the different beings have their own places: witches, for instance, are connected to old houses in forests; kelpies are in waterfalls; the Broonie in old mills and old buildings, and fairies have their fairy hills. And the Travellers say in their cracks and tales and stories that the fairies are shut up under the hills all winter, for nine months of the year.

When it comes to the first of May, the King of the Fairies lets them loose, sets them free for three months to do as they please. And they do plenty, you believe me! Nobody hardly ever sees any fairies, but the proof is there. They work among flowers and work among plants, helping Mother Nature. And at the end of July the fairies are gone. But they are so excited when they are set free at the beginning of summer. They have their party, their ceilidh, and lucky is the person who is in this very place on the first of May!

The old tramp was weary and tired, for he had walked all morning along the dusty highway, which in these days was just a track across the country. He had travelled for many days and come across very few places where he could find any food. All he'd had for the last two days was a rabbit he'd found by the roadside, roasted over a fire.

He said to himself, "If I don't find some habitation, a farm or a croft or something along the highway before nightfall, I'm sure I'm going to be very hungry." Because these old tramps begged whatever they could, whatever they needed to eat. It was only by the kindliness of the local people along the way that these tramps managed to survive. And he'd travelled for so many miles his feet were sore... the day was hot and the sun was shining. It was a beautiful summer day. Even suppose he was so hungry, tiredness began to overcome the hunger.

And then he came down by this little hill. Beside the roadside he looked across the moor and there was the most beautiful little hill he'd ever seen, covered in daisies and flowers. He said to himself, "Wouldn't that be a nice place to have a rest if I could afford to rest!" The hunger pains in his stomach were bothering him, but the soreness of his feet overcame them.

He walked over to the little hill and he sat down. He stretched himself out to rest and thought, in such a lovely place, if a person wasn't so hungry...

He'd rested for a long while, three-quarters of an hour or so, when all in a moment he heard a little voice saying, "Old man, you'll have to be gone from this place."

And the tramp looked around saying to himself, "Am I hearing right? Is there someone talking?" He looked all around – he could see nothing because the grass was high and the flowers were beautiful.

Then the voice spoke again, "Old man, you'll have to leave here!"

And the tramp looked again... Sure enough, there stood aside him a little man – not very big, maybe, say, twelve inches high with a long white beard and a peaked cap and peaked shoes. The tramp was amazed because he had never seen anybody... he'd heard of people so small as that many, many years before, but he'd never experienced meeting one. He couldn't hardly speak for a moment or two, he was so amazed.

Then he found his voice. "Little man," he said, "I am tired!"

And the little man said, "Old man, look, you must move from this place immediately!"

And the old tramp man said, "But who are you, little man? I have never seen anyone like you before."

The little man said, "Never mind who I am," and he came closer to the old tramp man.

When he came a little closer the old tramp man had to bend over and look down. The old tramp had pulled up his knees to himself and the little man hardly came as high as his knee… there he stood with his long white beard and his wee cap and curled shoes. And the tramp thought in his mind, this is queer, this is very funny. He was so tired and weary, but with the excitement of seeing this little creature the hunger in his belly was forgotten about.

And the little man said, "Old man, you'll have to move!"

The old tramp said, "Look, I am an old tramp. I am weary. I have come a long, long way and I am hungry. I have come here to rest." Now in these days a long time ago there were no fences along the way, no hedges; there were no roads. A person could walk off the track and sit down, rest theirself anywhere. So this is what the old tramp had done. He said to the little man, "Look, there's no reason why – that I can't rest here – because this is a free place. I'm enjoying myself on this little hill resting myself!"

And the little man said, "You must go!"

The tramp said, "Not tonight, I can't go another step!"

Then the little man saw he couldn't persuade him in any way. He said to the tramp, "What would you take to move on? Is it food you want?"

And the tramp said, "Not exactly food. My feet are sore, and food wouldn't make my feet any better."

The wee man looked down and saw the poor old tramp's boots were worn right through to the soles, with his toes sticking out. And the little man said, "I see your feet really are in a sorry state."

"Yes," said the old tramp, "my feet are in a sorry state and they're really sore."

So, the little man felt sorry for the tramp. He didn't argue or command him any more. He asked, "Old man, what would you really take to move from here?"

And the old tramp said, "Why is it so important I should move from here at this very moment?"

But the little man did not answer. "Well," he said, "what would you really take to move from this hill?"

And the tramp said, "Well, I am hungry, the pains are bothering my stomach at this moment. And I would like to go on to the next village or the next house or farm where I could find something to eat. But my feet are so sore and my boots are so worn the pain overcomes my hunger."

So the little man said, "If you had a nice pair of boots that made your feet comfortable, would you move on?"

The tramp said, "If I had some nice comfortable boots for my feet, I would surely be gone!"

The little man said, "Just wait a minute – I will find you some boots."

Now the old tramp in his hunger thought he was dreaming. He thought he had fallen asleep. He looked around and the little man was gone, completely disappeared. He rubbed his eyes with his hands and thought, I must have dozed over, I must have been dreaming. And he looked around the little hill; all the flowers were blooming so beautifully. He thought to himself, I'll just spend the night here, relax and have a sleep. Because these old tramps always slept out in the open. They had no home or no place to go.

But he hadn't waited more than three to four minutes, when back comes the little man. And over his back he had a pair of boots. The tramp looked, saw the little man with the boots and said, "I am not dreaming, I have not been asleep!"

And lo and behold, the little man came up beside his knee. But the boots were just small things. The little man said to the tramp, "I have brought you some boots and I hope you will keep to your promise."

But the tramp said, "Little man, I don't know where you came from, but do you realise that these boots would never fit my feet in any way – they wouldn't even fit my little toe!"

And the little man said, "Wait, just wait and watch!" The little man looked at the tramp's feet, saw his old boots with holes in them and his toes sticking through. He measured the size that the old tramp's feet really were, and he placed the boots down on the ground. He waited.

And the tramp watched. The boots got bigger and bigger and bigger – till they came about the size that the tramp really needed – and then they stopped. The tramp looked.

There before him were the most beautiful boots he had ever seen in his life. Many's the time the tramp had seen gentlemen and lairds and people of high degree with beautiful boots which he admired, but he had never owned a pair in his life. His one ambition in life was to own a beautiful pair of boots, because these tramps walked many, many miles.

Then the tramp said, "I just can't believe it! Are these for me?"

And the little man said, "Yes, they're for you! Old man, they're for you. You can have them with good heart and good will," he said, "providing that you try them on your feet and move on from this little hill immediately!"

The tramp bent down and took off his old boots, which were worn and dusty, no laces – a piece of lace tied across the centre – and his toes sticking out at the front, holes in the soles. He put them down. Then he stretched out his feet and picked up one boot that the little man had brought. He put it on his foot and it just fit perfectly! Then he picked up the other one, put it on, and it fit perfectly.

And the tramp stood up. When he stood up, the pain of his feet were gone. He wanted to be on his way, he felt so free! His hunger pains were gone, he just wanted to walk on.

But he could not walk away. He bent down, as close as he could above the little man and said, "Little man, I am thankful for what you've done for me."

And the little man said, "Do your feet feel good now?"

He said, "They feel wonderful. They feel wonderful!"

And the little man said, "Could you walk now, old man?"

He said, "Walk? I could walk for miles! I'll be on my way and leave you in peace."

But the little man said, "Stop!"

And the tramp said, "Why?"

"Oh, don't go away right now," said the little man.

The tramp was a wee bit worried because he thought the little man was going to take the boots back from him.

And the little man said, "Before you go, I want you to make me a promise!"

The tramp thought, make a promise? "I'll make you a promise," said the tramp. "What is your promise?"

The little man said, "Listen very carefully, because I'm going to tell you something."

And the tramp listened.

The little man said, "Now, you have got some boots."

The tramp said, "Yes, I have got some boots, some beautiful boots like I never had before in my life. I've seen people with boots but not anything like this! And I've admired people's beautiful boots along the way but I never saw boots like this before in my life. And are they really mine?"

And the little man said, "Yes, they're yours. But make me one promise! These boots will carry you on your journey for evermore, till the end of your life. They'll never need to be cleaned, they'll never wear, they'll never be worn out. You'll never have sore feet any more – providing on one thing…

"And what is that?" said the old tramp.

"*That you never tell a soul where you got them!* Will you promise me that?"

The old tramp turned round to the little man and he said, "I make you my promise."

And the little man held out his hand. The tramp took the little man's hand – just a wee, wee hand in his – and he shook hands with the little man.

"Now," said the tramp, "I'll be on my way. Can I go?"

"Well," said the little man, "you can go."

And the old tramp walked on the road, never even looked back, left the little man on the little hill by himself. The tramp went on his way. He felt no pain in his feet and no hunger pains. He just wanted to walk on and on, for ever! He travelled on for miles and miles and he travelled for a year, he travelled for two years… And wherever the old tramp went every night he took off his boots, and placed them beside his head when he went to sleep. And when he woke up in the morning his beautiful boots were there beside him as clean and polished like they had never ever walked a single step! And the tramp loved these boots like he had never loved anything in his life. Although he had walked many, many miles, the tramp never felt tired.

So, one day the summer came again. He came to this river. And the sun was shining; the day was so beautiful. The old tramp thought – he wasn't tired and his feet weren't sore – but he thought his boots were so beautiful, he was ashamed when he put his dirty feet in them. So he thought he'd walk down to the river and wash his feet – to fit his boots! He walked down to the river, took off his beautiful boots and placed them by his side.

He was washing his old feet in the river, cleaning his toenails so's he could put them back into his beautiful boots and feel no shame… when who should come walking up the river but a fisherman, who was fishing the river from pool to pool, from pool to pool. He came to the pool where the old tramp was sitting. And the fisherman was amazed when he came up and saw the old tramp washing his feet.

But he stopped and said, "Hello, old man!"

The old tramp looked round: there was the fisherman with his fishing bag on his back and his fishing rod. He said, "Hello!"

"You're washing your feet?" said the fisherman.

"Yes," said the tramp, "I'm washing my feet. Because the day is hot."

And then the fisherman looked. Beside the old tramp sitting was a pair of boots, the most beautiful boots that the fisherman had ever seen in his life! Then he looked at the tramp in rags, torn coat, long beard, straggly hair – and beside him sat the most beautiful boots he'd ever seen.

"Tell me," said the fisherman, "are you a tramp?"

"Well," said the old man, "people call me that. I have walked many, many miles – I am a tramp."

"I suppose," said the fisherman, "you've been many places?"

"Yes," said the old man, "I've been many places."

"And you've seen many sights?"

"Yes," said the old tramp, "I've seen many sights."

"But, tell me truthfully," said the fisherman, "how in the world could an old tramp like you own such beautiful boots?"

And the tramp turned round and smiled. "These boots," he said, "they be mine."

"But," the fisherman said, "you've after told me you're a tramp!"

"Yes," said the old man, "I'm a tramp."

"But, how," said the fisherman, "could a tramp own these boots, so beautiful like that? Did you steal them?"

"No," said the tramp, "I never stole them. They're mine!"

"Did you buy them?" said the fisherman.

"No," he said, "I never bought them. These were given to me as a present."

The fisherman said, "Look, I've never seen boots like that before. These boots are fit for a king – never mind a tramp!"

Then the tramp said, "They were made for a king; they were made for a king a long time ago. They were made for the King o' the Fairies! And the fairies were so kind to me because I landed on their little hill and they wanted me to move on, they gave me their boots."

The fisherman said, "The fairies? And the Fairy King? Ha-ha-ha!" And he picked up his rod and he walked on. The tramp watched him while he walked up the river.

Then the tramp turned round and he looked – his boots were gone mysteriously disappeared. And then it dawned on him: he had broken his promise to the little man. He was so sad! His boots, the most beautiful boots that had carried him so many, many miles, were gone. He sat and he sat for a long, long time and he knew in his heart there was no solution to his problem. The fairies had gifted him the boots to move from the little hill because they were going to have a fairy party there.

So he had to get up and walk on his way in his bare feet, till some poor crofter or some poor farmer took pity on him and gave him a pair of old boots. But to the end of his days the old tramp never saw his boots again, because he had broken his promise to the little man who had given him the boots of the Fairy King.

And that is the end of my story.

I heard this story a long time ago in Furnace when I was about twelve years old. I think I first heard it from a cousin of my father's, an old man called Willie Williamson whose brother stayed in Carradale.

JOHNNY MCGILL AND THE FROG

Nobody knew where Johnny McGill came from. Johnny was a wandering vet who just lived like a Traveller. Mary, his wife, walked with wares from door to door and sold things from her basket. She was a fortune-teller. But Johnny had no ambition in the world. Johnny didn't want to own anything or have any riches. His one love in life was looking after animals – all kinds, birds, the very mice, rats, anything that walked on four legs – Johnny McGill took care of. There were seagulls and crows with broken wings, even fish he was known to cure. He set out in his life to take care of all the little creatures who could not take care of themselves. Once on a camping place Johnny never left till the sick animal he was tending was as right as rain.

Oh, there's some great stories about Johnny McGill! The things Johnny did always turned out good for him. All the little creatures he sorted had a way of paying Johnny back, and Johnny said that it was in more important things than money.

One morning Johnny and his old wife were walking along as usual, with a little handcart, travelling on to no one knows where, wherever they could find a nice resting place by the roadside. Johnny had picked up a few things on his travels, a bird with a broken wing and little creatures he had mended on his way while his old wife sat patiently. And he let them go. But the ones who were seriously damaged he always carried with him.

So, the place they came to this morning was an old farm track, and Johnny was pushing his small handcart along when he stopped. And his wife who was beside him, Old Mary, wondered why he had stopped so suddenly. For there before them Johnny saw a common frog. And Johnny could see that the frog had been tramped on either by some cattle beast or by a horse or a rider who had paid no attention. But Johnny's eyes had seen that it was in trouble. So, he bent down quietly to pick up the frog.

Mary said, "Johnny, what are ye doing?"

He said, "Mary, my dear, it's a frog."

She said, "I know, Johnny. But it's just a frog."

"Oh, Mary, it might be just a frog to you but," he said, "it's another creature to me. Ye know, Mary, they all feel pain and they all suffer. But no one pays much attention to them, do they?"

So, he picked up the frog and he could see that one of its hind legs was broken. Johnny said, "Mary, it won't cause any trouble. I'll just take it along with us till we find the next camping place."

So, he put the frog on his little handcart in a safe place where it would not fall out and he travelled on. He hadn't gone far when he came to a little spot along the roadside which was derelict ground.

"Johnny," said Mary, "we'll stay here tonight."

He said, "I dinna see any fire marks. There's no been any Travellers around."

Johnny was always interested in the Travelling community, though they were not interested in him very much. They were kind of dubious about him because he was so clever and not one of their kind. And Johnny McGill was a great reader. So, he pulled in his little handcart, put up his tent, kindled his fire and Mary made some supper. So they sat and talked for a while.

Then Johnny said, "Mary, I've something to do." And he got to his frog: he took it, examined the frog all up and down, across its leg. He said, "Little fella, yer leg's broken. Ye're no good like that, ye'll never hop again unless we do something for ye. But don't worry, little friend, I'll soon fix ye." So, he set very carefully with some thread and some matchsticks, he bound and set the frog's leg.

"Now," he said, "little fella, ye'll be okay. My old wife and me has travelled far this last two weeks, and we'll just sit here and rest for a while, unless the police come along and move us on." Which the police seldom ever did to Johnny McGill because he was well known in the West Coast.

Johnny stayed there for two weeks attending to his frog while old Mary called the houses, sold her clothes pegs, leather laces and anything she had from her little basket. She told fortunes and she was quite happy. Johnny attended to many little creatures forbyes his frog. But one evening they sat up late in their little tent, and all the light they had, because it was near wintertime, was a candle. Johnny was reading from a book, and because he was tired he had placed the frog by his feet in a little box. Then, he got tired reading his book and he placed it by his side. He quietly dozed over to sleep.

But, unknown to Johnny the candle burned down. And there was some straw scattered around inside the tent which they used as a cushion for their bed. And the straw became alight... but Johnny was asleep. Then, as you know, Johnny lay naked from the waist. When something cold jumped on his chest! And he sat up with a start. He wakened, he looked all around – the straw by his bedside was on fire! Johnny clasped one hand to his breast, and with the other hand he put out the fire. Then he turned around and on his hand was the frog.

"Little fella," he said, "you're jumping again. And you've saved my life! I could have been burnt to death only for you – your coldness wakened me. Why did you jump on me? I know why you jumped on me: you wanted to tell me the tent was on fire. And now because you've jumped, I see that your leg must be better."

So, Johnny sat up there on his bed, and he quietly unrolled the thread from the frog's leg and the matchsticks and he tested it. He found that the bone had mended completely.

He said, "Little fella, ye're all right now," and he placed him by his bedside and went back to sleep.

In the morning when he awoke he sat up, said, "Mary, it's time to make some tea, breakfast time."

Mary got up quickly, washed her face, washed her hands, made some breakfast, filled her basket, said, "Johnny, are we staying here today?"

"No, Mary," he said, "I think we'll move on, because I see that my little friend has gone."

That's one story from my collection of Johnny McGill.

THOMAS THE THATCHER

Many, many years ago, hundreds of years ago, when there were no police or anyone to take care of the law and one thing and the other in wee villages, a man looked after the village and they called him a "burghmaster". And he held court out in front of his house. If anybody had any grievances or arguments to settle they came to the burghmaster and laid their disputes before him. He settled all the arguments, he was the master of the village.

In this village, it wasn't very big, there lived an old man called Thomas and he was the thatcher. He thatched all the roofs for the people of the village and he was known far out the land as the finest thatcher in the country. And when he went and did a job it was just immaculate – nobody could beat him at his job. His name spread far and wide as "Thomas the Thatcher". If he had another name nobody knew it.

So, one day the burghmaster is sitting at the front of his house when up comes two-three people from the village.

"Good morning, gentlemen!" he said.

"Good morning," they said, "Master. We have come to lay a complaint."

"Oh, aye," he says, "come in! Come in, sit down, men. What is your complaint?"

"We want to lay a complaint against Thomas the Thatcher," one said.

"Come, come, come! A complaint against Thomas the Thatcher?" he said. "I hope ye're no complaining about his work."

"Oh, no, no, no, Master," they said. "We're no complaining about Thomas's work," one said. "It's not his work."

"Well, I hope not," said the master. "Because he was here the day before yesterday, and look at my roof – look at my shed and the way – Thomas is the greatest thatcher in the world!"

"Yes," they said, "Master, we know that. But, we're here to complain about Thomas's *own* roof. The roof of his own house is in a terrible mess. And the thatch is all blown off with the wind. It's scattered high and low. It gets in wir feet, it gets in wir walks, it gets in wir gardens and he'll not do a thing about it. So, we want to charge him, lay a complaint so that you will get him to sort his roof and it won't be a nuisance to us any more!"

"Well, gentlemen," he says, "it's the first complaint I've ever had against Thomas the Thatcher. But it is a complaint. Thomas will be called to court tomorrow in front o' me, and I'll see his roof won't trouble you any more. Good day, gentlemen!" Off the men go.

So, the next day was court day. And Thomas was sent for, called in front of the burghmaster. And he came up along with the rest of the folk to hear the charges against him. So, he sat and he heard all the charges till it would come his turn. And he was called before the burghmaster.

"Thomas," he said, "I have a charge against you."

"Well, master," he said, "what is the charge? I have hurt no one."

He said, "You have hurt no one, but it's your roof, Thomas. You're known as the finest thatcher in the land and you do your work better than anyone we've ever known about. You work for me or work for anyone in the village. Every roof is so tidy – except yours! Why is your roof in such a mess compared to everybody else's roof, and you are a thatcher? I want you to tell me why your roof is not like the rest of the roofs that you work on."

So, Thomas walked up. He stood in front of the master and his head was bowed. "Master," he said, "it's not me. It's my friends."

"Come, come now, Thomas," he said, "we're all your friends. We're all your friends here. You mean to say it's us?"

"No, no, not you, master," he said. "My *little* friends," he says, "my friends of the air – the birds."

"What's about the birds, Thomas?" he said. "It's not the birds that's doing it, is it?"

"No, master, it's not the birds," he says. "But your roof and every roof in the village is pegged down with ash pegs, as I did myself and made your roofs tidy and neat. But there's not one single place in your roof where a bird could lie and could sleep for the night, and keep out of the cold air, is there? I leave my roof like that for my little friends to shelter in. I could tidy up my roof and peg it down and make it beautiful like your roof or anyone else's roof, but where would my little friends go in the wintertime, master?"

The burghmaster stood up. But before he could say another word – all these birds came down. And they gathered round old Thomas.

He says, "Come, come now, children, don't cause any disturbance with the people! You've got a complaint against me already, I don't want any more."

So, the burghmaster stood and said, "Thomas, you are a man, no only a thatcher but a man, a *real* man. In fact, you're the best man in this village. And I want you to know that. You go, Thomas, and take your little friends with you, and you leave your roof as it is and let them have shelter. We of this village never gave it a thought that a bird needs somewhere to sleep in the wintertime, we only thought of wirselves. And gentlemen," he said, if I ever hear of another complaint against Thomas the Thatcher as long as he's alive, I'll punish the complainer like I've never punished another man before in my life."

So, old Thomas went away and he took his birds with him. His roof remained like that for many's and many's a year… until Thomas died.

And when he died the villagers built a little statue for him made of iron, metal, of an old man kneeling feeding birds. So, if ever you're somewhere in a wee village in the East and ye come across a forgotten cemetery, and ye see a statue of a rusty old man feeding birds, you'll know that that was Thomas the Thatcher.

And that's the end of my wee story.

I heard this story from an old man called Johnny Townsley, a cousin of my mother's. Where the story originated I don't know; it could be a German or Flemish story. Some of my forebears probably heard it when they were abroad serving in the army. This is one way a story can be passed from place to place.

LEGEND OF THE WHITE HEATHER

W hy the white heather is lucky goes back many, many years...

There once lived a laird who had a great estate and he was dearly loved and respected by his own people, the villagers and his workers. He only had one fault – he didn't believe in good luck or wasn't superstitious in any way. When the men went on a boar hunt or a deer hunt all the women of the village would come out, and offer good luck charms to protect the men from getting attacked by a wild boar or falling off their horses.

But the laird would just laugh and scorn them, "Children!" And the thing was, he was the finest hunter among them and always came off best at the hunt. Till one day.

They were going on another boar hunt. As usual the ladies came and offered their men charms, which they accepted.

This one, the oldest woman of the village came to the laird, "Why don't you take something with you, sir, to bring you luck?"

He says, "Old woman, I don't need anything to bring me luck. I've never needed anything in all my days and I don't think I'll need it now. I don't believe in these things!"

She says, "Take a good luck charm with you, sir, you'll probably need it!"

"Not me," he said to the old woman, "I never bother about these things."

So they set on their way, all the huntsmen with their hounds to hunt the boar. And after they had gone a long way there rose a great black boar. They all set after it. But the laird got lost and landed by himself.

Then he got on the track of the boar and got it cornered. It charged his horse. The horse reared. And he was right on the face of a cliff, a steep cliff with a drop of hundreds of feet. When his horse reared up he fell off and rolled right over the cliff face, dropped twenty or thirty feet.

He's trying to get any kind of stone or something… when he grips this bush, a large bush. He's hanging on! And it took his weight. He started to shout for help. For at least half an hour he must have hung on afraid the bush was going to give way from the face of the cliff. But it took his weight still. Some of the men heard him shouting and they came to the cliff face. They lowered down ropes and rescued him.

When he came up he was all frightened and shaking, "I thought my time had come," he said. "If it wasn't for that bush I would have plunged right over the cliff."

And one of the men said, "Sir, that wasn't a bush. That was a sod of heather."

So he told one of the men, "Well, you go back down there and bring me up a piece of that heather! It saved my life. I want to take it home with me."

So a man was lowered down with a rope. He took a sod of the heather and brought it up. And what he brought up to the laird was white, white heather. The laird fetched it back to his castle and told the gardener he wanted it put right at his front door. Next morning everyone came and admired the laird's white heather at the front of his mansion. They were thankful that it had saved their master's life.

Each year it spread and got bigger till the laird was able to give everyone a piece of it. Everyone who got a piece of that heather kept it, and then gave a piece to somebody else. The luck of the white heather spread far and wide. Till today it's spread over three parts of the world!

But that's where the legend of the white heather came from, and that's a very old, old story.

HOUSE OF THE SEVEN BOULDERS

Away in the West Coast there is a ruins of a great house, and today it is known as the House of the Seven Boulders. But in bygone times it was not known by this name... because in this great house there lived an old woman who was said to have magical powers. And she had seven great warrior sons. They raided far across the land, stole and robbed, and everyone was powerless against these sons of hers. The king soon got tired of them raiding across the land. He sent armies to try and capture them, but they were great warrior swordsmen – no less than giants these men! His army would return bloody and battered from having a battle because they had to pass through a narrow gorge that led to the great house where they lived. And when these seven brothers held that pass no one could ever get through, and there was no way to the house except through this narrow pass.

There they lived with their mother, and from there they raided far and wide. The king had tried many, many times to capture these great brothers, but without success! He offered a large reward to anyone who could rid him of the warriors who raided across his lands, but no one could do anything to beat these brothers.

Now, the king had one daughter who was a young maiden of only eighteen years old. And she saw that her daddy was upset when word came again to his palace, the warriors had been out once more raiding. She saw that there was no way her daddy was going to get help of any description from anyone.

So, one evening she turned to him and said, "Father, why don't you let me help you against these great warriors?"

He says, "You, my dear? And what could you do against these warriors? I've sent my armies, I've sent troops and they've returned beaten and bloody and battered. I've offered a large ransom to anyone who could help me. And no one seems to help me. What could you do?"

"Please, Father," she said, "let me go! There must be something I can do."

He said, "My dear, I love you! You're my only daughter. There's no way in the world I'm going to let you out of my sight – never mind let you go up where there live these great warriors!"

She says, "Please, Father, I can help, I know I can help!"

Well, the king finally considered this for a long time. He'd do anything to get rid of these warrior swordsmen. He said, "How would you go about it?"

"Well," she says, "I would need help."

"Well" he says, "there's no help I can give you!"

She says, "Father, I don't want any help from you. I'll go and see my friend, the old henwife. She will help me."

Now, not far from the palace there lived an old woman who was a henwife. And she, too, was known to have magical powers. She was a great friend of the princess, ever since she was a child. And the princess had visited her many times. So, this day she took off to visit the old henwife, and she explained to her what she wanted to do. And the old henwife was very sad to hear her mention that she would even try and go and do something about these warriors.

She said, "My dear, what can you do? There's nothing really you can do."

She says, "Please, Mother," as she called the old henwife, "help me! You're the only one… my father is upset and he just can't go on like this. He's so unhappy when he hears word of these men raiding across his land, across his kingdom."

"Well," says the old woman, "there's only one thing I could do. I can't really help you to get rid of the warriors, but I can tell you what to do." She said, "Look, you know what a goose girl is?"

And the princess said, "Yes, I've heard of goose girls."

"Well," she says, "Look, I'll dress you as a goose girl and I'll give ye some geese. Then you make your way to the home of the warriors, and there you'll be on your own. Because they tell me their mother is a very kindly soul, even though they say she has magical powers. And maybe she will help you."

So, it was arranged that the next day the princess would dress herself as a goose girl, with her bare feet and a ragged dress and her staff. She would drive some geese across the land till she came to the gorge that led to the home of the great warriors. The young princess told her father the plan she had in mind. And he was very upset. He thought in his mind he would never see his little daughter again – if she was captured by the great warriors.

But she said, "Father, have no fear. I'll be able to take care of myself."

So, the very next day the young princess said goodbye to her father. She dressed herself as a goose girl in a ragged dress and plaited her hair in two plaits down her back. With her stick and her twelve geese she set off across the land. She travelled for many days doing her best, as the old henwife had told her, to sell some geese and swap some geese, to give away a female and receive a male goose from people along the roadway. Till finally she made her way to the narrow pass that led to the home of the great warriors, to the great house. And there she walked through the pass driving her geese, and no one stopped her. Till she came to the great house, and her geese began to eat round the front of the house. And she went up to the great house and she knocked on the door.

Lo and behold, it was opened by a tall old woman. She had never seen a woman so tall in her lifetime. The old woman herself was nearly seven feet tall!

And she bent down and she said, "Little one, what are ye doing here?"

And the princess said, "Ma'm, I'm just a goose girl, and I was wondering if ye're needing any geese?"

"Oh," she said, "needing any geese, my dear? I don't need any geese. My sons bring me everything I need. But if they find you here, your life is in danger."

She says, "Please, help me, I'm hungry and tired."

So, the old woman said, "The first thing we have to do…" The old woman was glad to have female company because she'd spent her life by herself and had never seen a human being like her, a woman like herself or a girl for many, many years. She only lived her life with these great sons of hers. And she was happy to see the young girl.

She says, "First we must shut up your geese where my sons won't find them. They'll be home shortly." So, she locked the geese up in a little shed and she said, "Come with me!"

She led the young girl into the great house. There she sat her down and gave her something to eat.

"Now," she said, "my dear, if my sons return and find you here you'll be in terrible trouble." And then she heard the clashing of swords and the tramping of feet. The mother said, "They're coming home!" And she shut her in a small cupboard in the great hall. There the young princess sat in terror in the great hall in the cupboard.

Then, in walked these great seven sons of the old woman and arranged themselves along the great dining hall, and demanded their mother to feed them, bring them wine! So, the old mother fed them and brought them great flagons of wine. And then, they sat and drank and talked, boasted about their escapades across the land.

Then… the young girl sneezed with the dust in the cupboard!

And the oldest brother rose and said, "Mother, you've been deceiving us! There's someone here!" And he ran to the cupboard. He opened it and there stood the young goose girl, the princess. He put his hand in and pulled her out. He said, "Brothers, look what I have found!" And he brought her forth. He said to his mother, "Where did she come from?"

And the mother said, "It's only a goose girl. Leave her alone!"

He said, "A goose girl here or a goose girl there – she's a young handsome woman! And one of us must have her."

The seven brothers started passing the young princess from each to the other, all demanding that *he* wanted her! And the old woman could not take this.

She ran from the great dining hall out to the front door of the house. Then she clapped her hands and cried, "Bring your swords, we're getting invaded!"

And the seven brothers grabbed their swords and ran out the front door to see who was invading them. And the young princess sat in terror.

Then, there was quietness…

And the old woman walked in and she said, "My little dear, you can come up now." The young princess was sitting on the floor. "You can come up now, my dear, everything's all right. They'll never bother you again."

The young girl said, "Where have they gone, Mother?"

She says, "Come with me and I'll show you. They'll never trouble you or anyone again." And she led the princess to the great front door. There before the door stood seven great boulders, each one weighing over three ton, right beside the door of the house. She turned to the little goose girl.

"I know why you came here, my dear. You are not a goose girl. You are the daughter of the king, you are a princess! And you have come to rid the land of my sons. Well," she says, "it was time the world was rid of them, not just the land. Because they've been causing too much trouble, and I would never let them harm you."

And the young princess said to the old woman, "Yes, I am the princess, Mother. I came to try and help my father the king to rid the land of these great warriors of yours."

The old woman said, "Well, my dear, you can go home to your father now and tell your father they will never bother him again, because they are gone."

And the princess said, "The only way I'll go back, Mother – if you will come with me and be my companion for the rest of my life." Because she wasn't really a very old woman.

So, the next day the little princess and the old woman said goodbye to the great house and walked away to her father's kingdom. And the king was happy to hear that the great warriors were gone for ever. And the princess had a great companion.

But, as years passed by the house became derelict. The roof fell in and the walls began to fall down. The House of the Seven Boulders became overgrown with grass and trees and thorns and branches. And it came to pass that people could no more explain why anyone would have seven large boulders at the very door of their house... But these were the seven great warrior sons who were transformed to stones by their own mother.

That is a legend that is true.

This story was told to me a long time ago by an old cousin of my father's called Willie Williamson. God rest his soul, he died when he was ninety years old in the old people's home in Campbeltown, Argyll. And this was one of his favourite stories. It happened a long, long time ago.

THE BROONIE ON CARA

Down near Campbeltown in Argyll there's a wee island called Cara; Carrie is what the local folk say. And the local villagers believe that that is the home of the Broonie – he stays on Cara. The island is small and there's only one house on it. There's water on Cara – you can walk down the steps cut out of stone to the Broonie's Well, where he's supposed to drink his wee drop water. But otherwise Cara is uninhabited.

Now many years ago a minister, who was a great believer in the Broonie, bought the wee house on Cara and he and his wife moved out to the island. They lived very happily on Cara and they took a cow across with them to supply them with milk. The minister loved the island, he set lobster pots and fished, he was quite happy and contented. He had no family, just him and his wife.

So the minister had a boat and he used to travel across to Bellochantuy when he needed to go to Campbeltown for his messages. In these days it was only a track to Campbeltown, just a horse track; it was all done by pony and trap. Once a week he had to go across to the mainland to give a service in Campbeltown. He drove by pony and trap and always took his wife with him when he went. They would row their boat across from Cara, tie it up, borrow a pony and trap from a local farmer and drive to Campbeltown, do his service in the church and drive back, leave the pony and trap at the farm and row across to Cara to his house. But one morning it was a beautiful Sunday morning, his cow was about to calf.

So he said to his wife, "I think we'll take the cow out." Now next to his house was a wee shed where he kept a wee byre for holding the cow. He took the cow out and said, "Poor soul, you're better walking about, it'll help ye when ye're going to have a calf, ye can walk about, for you seem very sick." He let the cow go.

He and his wife went down, took the boat, rowed it across, tied the boat up, took the pony and trap from the farmer and drove to Campbeltown, about fifteen miles. It's not far for a horse, a horse will do it in an hour and a half. He did his service in the church, came out of the church, talked to his friends, yoked the horse and left Campbeltown. But there came a storm, a terrible time of rain and wind.

He said to his wife, "Come storm or hail or rain, we'll have to get home tonight to Carrie."

But the weather got worse. He drove back the fifteen miles to Bellochantuy, then on to Muasdale. When he came to Muasdale the weather was still worse. You could hardly see – the rain was battering, the waves were lashing.

And his wife turned round to him, "Husband, we'll never get home tonight to Carrie, there's no way in the world that we're going to get across, take our own boat across to Carrie tonight!"

He says, "Wife, we'll have to. What about our cow, what's about the wee cow? It's out there itself wandering on the island the night among this rain and sleet!"

They drove the horse back to the farm, drove up to the house. The old farmer came out and met them. After the horse had been tied up and its harness taken off, the minister came in and had a cup of tea or a dram. The waves were lashing and the boom was coming across from Cara.

So the old farmer said to the minister, "Look, there's no way in the world you're going to cross that sea tonight, for the peril of your wife's life."

But the minister says, "What about my wee cow?"

He said, "Does the cow mean more to ye than your wife, or your own life?"

The minister said, "Look, the cow's wandering the night – I let her loose before I left."

The farmer finally persuaded the minister that there's no way in the world he was going to take a boat across that night to Cara. It was impossible!

Now the cow was on its own. The island is desolate, it's not very big, only about three acres, practically all rock. Not a soul is on the island, just the house, the byre and the cow – no dogs, no cats, nothing.

The minister was very unhappy but he stayed in the farm, the old farmer put him and his wife up for the night. He passed a terrible, sleepless night because he was thinking on his wee cow in the island on its own, wandering alone with the cold and the wind, and it was going to calf.

But anyway, morning came which it always does. And the minister was up bright and early. It was a beautiful day, the sea calm, the wind was gone, the rain gone, and there was hardly a wave to be seen. And he called his wife; he couldn't hurry quickly enough. They had a wee bit breakfast from the farmer and bade him goodbye, left the pony and trap for the farmer to take care of and hurried down across the road about four hundred yards from the farm, through a wee field down to the boat. The minister got in the boat and his wife got in the back. They were just a young couple in their thirties, no children. He got into the oars and pulled the boat across as fast as he could. And, och, the sea was as calm as the palm of your hand, not a wave, nothing. The sun was shining. He rowed across to Cara.

And right where you land the boat is a wee place in the rocks, there's a few steps which go down to the Broonie's Well, and water comes out of this rock face. The minister pulls in the boat and there's a bolt in the wall and a ring to tie up your boat. He tied the boat to the ring, couldn't hurry fast enough, helped his wife out of the boat. And the two of them hurried up the wee shingle path to the house. But before the minister went near the house he searched all around as far as he could see looking for the cow. Cow was gone.

He said to his wife, "She's probably been blown over the rocks and carried away in the tide."

Into the house the minister went. The wife made a cup of tea and he was sitting down in his chair completely sad and broken-hearted because he loved this wee cow dearly. It was the only thing gave them milk on the wee island. They loved the solitude and peace and quietness of this island, that's why they went there in the first place, because he could think about God and his sermons. He was a good man, a really good man.

He said to his wife, "I'm really sorry, look what happened. Well, I'll take a wee walk and walk around the shoreside, see if I can find the carcass of her. She was probably carried away with the tide."

But as he went outside he thought he'd have a last look in the byre where he used to tie the wee cow up at night-time. He said, "If I only had left her tied in the byre, she'd be safe." Now, he used to always fill a pail of water for the cow and carry it in, for there was no running water inside the wee byre. But before he had gone away Sunday morning, when he'd left the cow out on the grass – he had carried the pail outside. When he walked out the door of the house now, he looked at the door of the byre… the pail was gone. He said, "I remember, I took the pail out and left it at the door when I let the cow out."

There was nothing to do. He walked to the byre, opened the door and walked into the byre. There was the wee cow standing, a pail of water at her head, a beautiful heap of hay in the wee heck at her nose and the bonniest wee calf you ever saw standing at her feet. And the chain was round her neck; she was tied up, tied up to the stall where he had always tied her before. The minister stood and looked. He was aghast. He ran into the house, called his wife.

"Come out," he said, "I want to show you something!"

"What is it?" she said.

"Come here, come here. I want to show you something! Look!" he said to his wife. He opened the door of the byre and showed her – there was the cow and there was the bonnie wee calf standing at her feet. There was the pail of water and the hay in her wee heck at her nose, and the cow as healthy as could be and so was the calf! He turned round and told his wife, "Look, there's only one explanation," he said, "and you know as well as me… there was nobody on this island when me and you left."

"I know," she said to him, "Angus, there was nobody here when we left."

He said, "There's only one person responsible for this."

She says, "I know."

He says, "That was the Broonie."

And that man spent all his days on that island, till he became an old man when he retired to Campbeltown. He believed, and he was a man of the cloth, nobody in the world could convince him otherwise. It could not have been anybody but the Broonie who tied up his wee cow that night on the island of Cara.

And that's the last of my wee story.

The Broonie is a spirit that never dies. He can take any form if he wants to, but he comes in the form of the lonely old tramp with a ragged coat. A wee old tramp man, about five feet tall, with the wee white beard and the two blue eyes, the kindly old creature of a man who never insults, never hurts, is always looking for work and he's always hungry. His famous meal, he loves a bowl of porridge and milk, or a bowl of soup. It's something that goes back many, many years, long before your time and mine, about the supernatural being who was cast down to take care of us, the humble folk.

THE BROONIE'S FAREWELL

Many years ago there lived a small farmer on a hill farm in the West Highlands of Scotland. He and his wife had this wee farm between them. They were very poor off; they didn't have very much to start with. But as years went by he became a rich man, and when he was middle-aged he had a wee son. The mother and father loved this wee boy dearly. And his mother was such a kindly woman, she couldn't see anything going wrong with him; they gave up everything in the world they really needed for the sake of their son. And the son returned it every way possible. He was really good to his mother and father, helped in every way he could. If ever there was a job needing to be done about the place, he would always say, "Daddy, I'll do it."

His mother would say, "No, son, just dinna hurry yourself. Take your time and just help your daddy whenever possible."

So, it came a Saturday afternoon. By this time the laddie was about eleven years old. The old woman was sitting in the kitchen and she said, "Can you two men not find a job for yourselves? Because I'm going to bake."

And the father said, "Come on," to the laddie, "that's a sign that me and you are no wanted!"

So, they walked out of the house and he said, "Daddy, what are we going to do?"

"Well, son, I'll tell you what we're going to do." He said, "We've got everything done, hay's all cut, so we'll need to go in and clean up the barn because it's getting kind o' tottery. I'm beginning to fall ower things in the morning when I go in there."

113

"All right," said the wee laddie, "I'll go and get a wheelbarrow, Daddy, and we'll clean out the barn."

So, the wee laddie got a wheelbarrow, hurled it into the barn. And the man's picking up old bags and all kinds of stuff. He's putting it in the barrow. But, hanging behind the door of the barn inside was a coat and a pair of breeches and a pair of hose. They were covered in cobwebs.

The wee laddie reached up. "Okay, Daddy," he says, "here's some old clothes."

"Oh, no, son," he says, "no, don't touch that!"

"Why, Daddy," he says, "it's only old rags."

"No, son," he says, "it's not rags. While your mother's baking we'll keep out of her way, and we have not much to do in here, we're nearly finished… Sit down there and I'll tell you a wee story." So, the farmer took a pitchfork and raked up a bunch of hay, he made a seat.

"Now," he said to the wee boy, "sit down here, son, and I'll tell you about that coat, breeches and the hose…"

"Many years ago, long before you were born, when me and your mother came here, this place was pretty run down and we didn't have very much money. I got it at a very cheap rent. We came up here and we worked away hard, both your mother and me, and tried to make this place into a kind of decent farm. Well, we hadn't been here for over a year and things were really tough.

"And one night late, about the month o' October, your mother and I were sitting down to a wee meal, that we didn't have very much at that time, when a knock came to the door. And your mother said, 'Go and see who that is at this time of night.'

"So, naturally I went out, and there standing at the door was an old man."

"What kind o' man, Daddy?" the wee boy said. "What kind o' man was he?"

"Well," he said, "he was just an ordinary old man, but he

wasn't very big and he had a white beard. But he had the two bluest eyes that ever I saw in my life. So, I asked him what he wanted.

"He said, 'I'm just an old man and I thought you maybe have some work, or could give me shelter for the night.'

"So your mother shouted to me, 'Who is it, John?'

"'It's an old man looking for shelter.'

"'Well,' she said, 'bring him into the kitchen!'

"So, I said, 'You better…'

"'No, no, no,' he said, 'I can't come into the kitchen.'

"The old man wouldn't come into the kitchen even though your mother came to the door. And she coaxed him, but he wouldn't come, in any way.

"So, with your mother being a kind-hearted soul, she asked him, 'Are you hungry, old man?'

"'Oh,' he said, 'I'm hungry, yes, I'm hungry.'

"'Would you like something to eat?'

"'Oh, I would love something to eat. Could you give me a bowl o' porridge and milk?'

"And naturally, that's what me and your mother were having that night – porridge and milk. So, your mother filled a big bowl and I carried it out to him and gave it to him in his two hands.

"And I took him into the barn, I said to him, 'There, old man, you can find shelter for the night-time.'

"Well," the farmer said, "I put him in the barn, and," he said, "believe it or not what I'm going to tell you, that old man stayed with me for six months and I never saw a harder worker in my life. I had practically nothing to do round the place. He was up, first thing in the morning he started to work, to the last thing at night he was still working. He had everything about this place prospering like it never prospered before. I never lost an animal of any kind. I had the greatest crops that ever I could ask for and I came in and offered him wages, but he wouldn't have any. Or he wouldn't come into the house, all he wanted to do was sleep in the barn.

"Well, after working for about six months your mother took pity on him. And one night she sat down special herself and made him a coat because he was ragged. And she made him a pair o' breeches cut down from mine and she knitted him a pair o' hose. And one morning when she came out with his bowl o' porridge, she brought them and placed them beside his bowl. Later in the morning when I came out, the coat, the breeches and the hose were gone. And the bowl was empty – his old breeches and his coat were hung behind the door.

"And there they've been hung, son, for over eleven years. And *remember*: some day this farm will pass on to you but promise me, as long as you own this place, you'll never part with these breeches, or that coat or thae hose!"

"No, Daddy," he said, "I never will."

And when the man passed on and the young laddie got the farm, the breeches and the coat and the hose hung behind the door till it passed on to his son.

And that's the last of my wee story.

People were very privileged to be visited by the Broonie. And if he ever visited any place at any particular time, his visit was never forgotten. Word of it always passed down, from generation to generation, and this is where "The Broonie's Farewell" really came from. An old Traveller man told me this story a long time ago when I was very young. He said it really happened, he was supposed to have been at the farm – away back in the highlands of Argyllshire, near Rannoch Moor – I don't know the name of the farmer in the story. But the Broonie didn't care for anybody without a "Mac" in their name. The Broonie was the patron spirit of the MacDonalds.

The breeches the Broonie left in the barn were short, just came below the knee. The hose was pulled up to meet them. They laced down the side of the leg and were made of corduroy. They hung at the back of that door for years and years, and were never allowed to pass away from that place.

You're not to pay the Broonie, you see. You can thank him, but the minute you pay him, you're finished. He wouldn't take any money, and when she'd left the clothes down beside his bowl he thought: that's your payment – we've nae mair use for you...

He was gone. So, that's why the old man told the laddie to hang on to the coat. He thought maybe the Broonie might come back.

THE COMING OF THE UNICORN

Many, many years ago, long, long before your time and mine when this country was very young there wonst lived a king. But this particular king was a great huntsman, and he lived with his wife in this great castle. The only thing that this king really loved to do was hunt – small animals, big animals – and in these bygone days the land was overrun with animals! The king had his huntsmen and he had a beautiful wife, a beautiful palace and kingdom, and he was very happy. He got pleasure from hunting. But the king only hunted to supply food for his own castle and the villages around his kingdom. He used to go on hunts three-four times a year to give his people enough food.

But one particular day this king gathered all his huntsmen together. They said goodbye to the womenfolk because they'd be gone for a couple of days, maybe more, to bring back all these animals they would salt for the winter. He bade goodbye to his queen as usual and took all his huntsmen. They rode out.

They rode for many days in the forest, because in these bygone days it was mostly all forest. There were not many townships or little villages along the way. The land was desolate but overrun with animals of all description. Then the huntsmen always made sure that the king should get the best shot, anything that would come up before them. It was all bows and arrows in these days, and swords.

So, lo and behold what should stop before the king, what should they corner but a bear, a great brown bear! The huntsmen drew back and let the king have the first shot, because it was a big bear and they knew it carried a lot of weight, would be a lot of food for the villagers. The king who was a great archer, put his bow and arrow to his shoulder and fired. He fired an arrow and hit the bear; the arrow stuck in the bear's chest.

And the bear stood up straight when the blood started to fall from its chest. It put its paw to its chest where the arrow had entered, held it there for a few minutes.

And the king was amazed: it stood straight there and took its paw, looked at the blood on its paw and looked at the king. Then it cowpled over, fell down dead.

And the king was so sad at seeing this. He told his huntsmen, "Pick it up and carry it back. We will hunt no more today."

They carried the bear back to the palace and the king said to his huntsmen, "Take and divide it among the villagers, but bring me its skin."

So, naturally the huntsmen divided the bear up, passed it around to all the people in the village. And they brought the skin to the king. And the king gave orders for the skin to be dried. Through time the skin was dried, brought into the palace and put upon the floor.

But every time the king looked at the skin he got sadder and sadder. The sadder he got the less he thought about hunting. Now the next hunt was coming up the king did not want to go. He went into his chamber. The bugle was sounding, they called on their king! But lo and behold, the king would not go. And from that day on to the next months and the next months following, no more did the king join the hunt. His charger was waiting, his beautiful horses were in the stable, his bows and arrows sharpened; but the king never went. The king was downhearted, broken. The queen was upset.

"Why," she said, "what happened to Our Majesty the King? What is the trouble?"

The huntsmen told her, "He has the bearskin."

She removed the bearskin from the floor of the palace but it made no difference. The king had his meals, he had his lunch. He talked to the queen, talked to everybody, but he had seemingly lost all interest in life. He was a great sportsman and swordsman, but now he did not want to do anything. The queen was very upset. She could see her king fading away. He just wanted to sit in his parlour and be by himself.

So one day she could stand it no more. She called the three palace magicians, told them the story I'm telling you.

"Look, you must do something for the king. He doesn't cuddle me, make love to me, just sits there completely lost. You must do something to excite him, bring him back to his own way, make him a king once more! His people are worried; he has never put in an appearance before his people. He doesn't join the huntsmen – he is in another world – what has happened to our king?"

So the three wise men, the magicians of the palace, put their heads together and said, "We know his trouble. It was the bear, seeing the blood from the bear made him so sad he does not want to hunt any more. But if we could between us construct something that would excite him – make him be a king again – then everything would be all right."

So, the three court magicians put their heads together: "Well," they said, "what could we do to excite him?"

One said, "If we could construct an animal, a special animal, who would be swifter than the wind, fiercer than the lion and fiercer than a boar that everyone was afraid of – and we would beg the king to help us – then maybe we could bring him back from his doldrums and make him a king once more."

The three magicians were very wise men, very clever; they worked in magic in the king's court. They put their heads together and one said, "Well, I could use my power to give it the body of a pony who will ride and fly swifter than the wind."

And the second one said, "I could give it the fierceness and the tusk of a boar."

And the third one said, "I could give it the power and the tail of a lion."

So, lo and behold the three magicians constructed an animal between them: they gave it the beautiful slender body of the swiftest pony that ever rode on the earth. They gave it the tusk of a boar – but instead of putting it on its mouth they put it on his forehead. They gave it the determination of a lion and the power of the lion, but instead of giving it the lion's body they put the lion's tail on it.

"And what," did they say, "are we going to call it?"

"Well," one said, "we universt between us to construct it… we will call it a *unicorn*."

And there lo and behold became the birth of the unicorn – the most beautiful, the most wonderful – the swiftest and fiercest animal of all. These three wise men set it free to roam the kingdom, to interrupt every huntsman that ever went on their way.

So, naturally the huntsmen, who had got tired waiting for the king and tired waiting for food, knew that there was no way they could coax the king to go with them, went on the hunt without the king! But whenever they went to hunt up jumped before them this beautiful animal – white as white could be, a beautiful pony, the tail of a lion and the tusk of a boar straight from its forehead. And it ran before them. They hunted and they searched for it, but it was fiercest and attacked them, it threw them off their horses. But no way in the world could they hurt it, no way in the world could they catch it. So, after hunting for weeks and months, they finally rode back to the palace bedraggled and tired with not one single thing because of the interest to catch this animal.

When one of the old court magicians walked out and said to them, "What is your problem, men? Why have you come home from the hunt so empty handed?"

And they said, "We have come home empty handed because we could not catch anything. Because an animal we have never seen in our life – with a horn in its forehead, with the swiftness of a pony, with the fierceness of a lion and the tail of a lion – has come before us at every turn. And we tried to fight it but it was impossible."

"We must tell the king," said the court magician, "we must tell the king about this animal! Maybe it will get him out of his doldrums."

So they walked up, they told the king and they begged, "Master, Master, Master, dearest Huntsman, dearest King, Our Majesty, we have failed in our hunt and the people in the village are dying with hunger because we have no food for them."

"Why," said the king, "you are huntsmen aren't you? Haven't I taught you to hunt?"

"But, Majesty," they said, "it's an animal, this being, this thing that we've never seen in our lives. The swiftness of a pony and the horn on its head of a boar and the tail of a lion, who is as swift and so completely swift that drives before us, that we just can't catch it."

"There never was such a thing," said the king, "not in my kingdom!"

"Yes, Our Majesty," they said, "there is such a thing. He interrupts us and he interferes with our hunt, and every minute he disappears and then he's gone; we just can't go on with the hunt. And our people are dying with hunger. You must help us!"

But then said the king, "Is it true? Tell me, please, is there something that I've never seen in my kingdom?"

"Yes, Our Majesty," he said, "there is something you have never seen. This animal is bewitched!"

And at that the king woke up. He rubbed his eyes and the thought of the bear was gone from him for evermore.

He said, "If there is something that interrupts my people and interrupts my huntsmen, then I must find the truth!"

So the king calls for his horse, he calls for his bows and he calls for his arrows. He blows the bugle and calls for his huntsmen, "Ride with me," he says, "to the forest and show me this wonderful animal that upsets you all. It won't upset me!" And the king was back once more. And the people are happy, they blow their bugles; everyone gathered in the court to see the king off once more after a year. They rode out on the great hunt.

"Lead me," says the king, "to where you saw this animal last!"

So, they led him to the forest and the old wise men were sure that it was there. And *there* before him stood this magnificent animal, taller than any horse the king had ever rode, with a horn on its forehead and the tail of a lion, the swiftness of the wind.

And the king said, "Leave it to me!" It stood there and looked at them. The king said, "Leave it to me!" And the king had a great charger. He rode after it for many, many miles and the farther the king rode the farther it went. And the faster the king rode the faster it went, till it disappeared in the distance and then the king was lost. It was gone. Sadly and tiredly he returned to the sound of his trumpets of his huntsmen. But the king had never even got close enough to fire an arrow at it. For days and weeks and months to pass by the king hunted and the king searched for this beautiful animal, but it always disappeared in the distance. It always rose before him, but he could never catch it.

The king became obsessed with this animal – he only had one thing in his mind, that he must catch this animal. He called his great wise men and his court together. What kind of animal was roaming his kingdom? His huntsmen tried to explain.

"Master," said one of the great court magicians, "it is a *unicorn*!"

"A unicorn?" said the king, "how many unicorns are there on my land?"

And they said, "Only one, Our Master, and it's up to you to catch it."

But the king wasted his time. He searched for weeks, for months and took his huntsmen. The people were dying for food. But the king could never ever catch the unicorn. And then, when the king became so sad and broken-hearted he called his great men together.

He says, "Look, this is a magic animal. I know in my heart that I am a great huntsman. But I've done something that I should never have done, deprived all my people of food because we depend on the hunt. I have not killed a deer or killed a wolf or anything for months. But," he told his huntsmen, "you go out and hunt for food for the villagers, spread it among the people while I talk to my sculptors and my masons."

To them he said, "I know that I can never catch the animal they call a unicorn. But there is nothing in the world I could love more than just to have a statue of him at my door where I could walk and see him."

And they asked him, "Master, we don't know – what do you want?"

"Well," he said, "I will tell you and I want you to make it for me." So he explained to the sculptors and the masons, "It was like a pony with a tail of a lion and a horn on his forehead and the swiftness of the wind."

So, they carved him out of some stone. They carved from stone two things like the king had told them to be, and put them straight in front of the king's castle. So that every morning when the king walked down, there stood before him the thing that he hunted for many, many months, which he had never captured – the unicorn. The king loved to put his hand on his statues, two of them, one on each side of the door of his palace like a beautiful pony with a horn on his forehead and the tail of a lion. And he walked around them.

From that day on he hunted with his friends and distributed all the food that he ever found – deer, bears, foxes, wolves – he hunted the lot. But from that day the sculptors built the unicorns in front of his door he never saw his *unicorn* again.

But when the king passed on, for many years still remained what the sculptors had made in front of his palace. And that's where your unicorn came from today.

That is a true story and that is also the end of my tale.

THE KINGS' GARDENS

There are many stories about kings, especially kings of Scotland, but we know there were kings all over the world. And in my story, these two kings' names are steeped in history; we don't actually know for a fact where their countries were because the story is so old. But their countries bordered each other, and these two kings were great friends of each other. They had their armies, their soldiers, but they fought no wars against each other. Because they had something in common each loved – that was their gardens.

In their palaces they each had a walled garden, so that they could walk with their families and admire the beauty of nature. One of the kings was called the King of the West and the other the King of the East. Once a year they would meet at the border and discuss many things. But they would never, never invade each other's territory, because each of them loved their garden so much. If they had any spare time, they loved to be in their gardens with their families, not fighting wars. And the most important person in the palace was not the prime minister or the head of state; it was the local gardener, because they depended on him to keep the garden in perfect condition.

But one day the King of the West was walking in his garden admiring the beauty of the flowers and the bushes and trees when he had a strange thought in his mind: I wonder if my friend the King of the East has got his garden more beautiful than mine. He's invited me to visit many times but I've never accepted his offer.

And this began to trouble him, "Is his garden more beautiful than mine?" he said. And then he had an idea. Yes, he would go, for the peace of mind, he would send a messenger to the King of the East and tell the King of the East he was coming for a visit for the first time in his life.

So, a messenger rode off on horseback and was gone for some time, but many days later returned with a message from the King of the East: "Yes, my friend, please do come, you'll be more than welcome. Come and stay as long as you like. Bring your queen with you if you want and see my country."

But the queen of the King of the West was a little disabled and not allowed to travel with her husband.

So, accepting the offer, the King of the West took some couriers and soldiers with him, and for fifteen days he travelled to the kingdom of the King of the East. He was met there. The King of the East made him welcome and there was a great feast. They wined and dined, there was plenty food and drink, music and dancing for everybody. The King of the East was so pleased to see his friend from the West.

Then, some days later, turning to the King of the West, the King of the East said, "My friend, is there anything I could do for you before you return to your country, to your homeland?" And this was the opportunity the King of the West was waiting for.

He said, "Yes, my friend, I would love to see your garden. You see, I love my garden and you've told me many times about yours. Could I see it?"

"Of course, my friend," said the King of the East, "I will come with you and you can view my garden to your heart's content."

"No, no," said the King of the West, "let me go alone – I would like to see it by myself!"

So, the King of the East led him to the great iron gate. It swung wide and the King of the West stepped into the garden and he stopped in amazement. He gazed around him: here was the most beautiful garden in the world, nothing out of place, not a blade of grass, not a pebble. The trees were trimmed and beautiful, the flowers growing, the roses growing. It was the most beautiful place he had ever seen in all his life. And by seeing this he felt a little upset. His garden was not like this!

So, feeling rather sad, the next day he departed for his home, saying goodbye to his friend. And when he arrived home at his kingdom in the West, to his palace, the queen was there to meet him. She could see he was a little troubled.

She said, "Did you not enjoy yourself, my darling, on your travels to visit your friend?"

"Yes," he said, "I had a wonderful time, but you should see his garden! He's got the most beautiful garden in the world, far more beautiful than my garden will ever be. You see, my gardener wines with me and he dines with me. He is my friend and is supposed to look after my garden, but he's been deceiving me. Send for him!"

So, the gardener was sent for. He came before the king and said nothing.

And turning to him, the king said, "Gardener, as well you may know, I have just returned from my friend, the King of the East. I have been there for some time and viewing his garden. He's got the most beautiful garden in the world! You've been deceiving me. You're supposed to make me a beautiful garden so my family can enjoy it. And all these years you wined with me and dined with me... Why is my garden in such a mess compared to the King of the East's?"

The gardener said nothing.

And the king said, "For that, I'm going to send you to the dungeon."

The gardener was led away to the dungeons. The king sat. He repented for three days as the gardener lay in the dungeons without food or water. And then the king had a second thought.

He said, "It would do no good having my gardener lying in the dungeons. It wouldn't make my garden any better."

So, he gave orders for the gardener to be released. And so it was the gardener was brought before the king.

Turning to the gardener he said, "Gardener, I'm going to give you one more chance, I want you to make me a beautiful garden. Take as many workers as you want, but make me a garden that I can enjoy!"

"So be it," said the gardener, "it shall be done! But you shall not enter that garden for six months."

"Do as you please," said the king, "but make it beautiful."

So, the king was not allowed in his garden for six months and he gardener laboured and toiled.

When the six months were up, one morning he came to the king and said, "My lord, my sire, it is ready, you may walk in your garden."

The king said, "Let me walk by myself," and the king walked in, he stopped in amazement.

Here was beauty. There was not a pebble, not a blade of grass out of line, the trees were trimmed, the bushes were trimmed – it was the most beautiful garden in the world. But the king looked all around him. He stood there and felt very unhappy. He had the garden he'd asked for, but what was wrong with it? It was far more beautiful than the garden of the King of the East. But he could not fathom, what was wrong with his beautiful garden that took six months to make?

So, he called the gardener. And he says, "Gardener, I thank you for such a beautiful garden. But will you please tell me, why am I so unhappy with it? It's the most beautiful garden in the world, far superior to that of the King of the East, but I'm still unhappy, what is wrong?"

And the gardener said, "I will tell you, my king. You see, I left your garden – the way it was before – I left trees to twist, their branches to twist, so that the birds could come and build their nests and sing for you. I left the thistles in your garden so the little mistle thrush could come build its little nest and bring up little babies. I left the grasses and the weeds for the little hedgehog and the shrew, the weasel and the rabbit, all the little creatures that you could enjoy. But now they are gone. There's no place for them any more. You have a beautiful garden but the little ones are gone."

And this made the king feel very sad. He said, "Gardener, I thank you for such a beautiful garden. I'll see that you shall be rewarded handsomely. But please, please, please, could you do something for me? Would you make my garden the way it was to me before – so that I can enjoy the company of my little ones, so that the birds will sing for me once again?"

And the gardener said, "So be it, my king. But that garden gate shall be closed; no one shall enter the garden for one year."

"So be it," said the king, "I can wait."

So the great gate was closed, a padlock and chain was put across. No one entered the garden. And within the year the branches began to twist, they went round the bushes and trees. The grasses and weeds and thistles began to come up and one by one the little creatures found their way back into the king's garden to find sanctuary. The mistle thrush came back into the garden to build its nest in the thistles and sing, bring up its babies. The rabbit, the hedgehog, the shrew and all the little creatures made their home in the king's garden. The blackbird and the thrush came and built their nests in the twisted bushes of the garden that began to twist within the year.

One morning in early spring the gardener came before the king, "My lord, my sire, this morning you can walk in your garden."

And the great chain was taken off, the gate swung wide and the king stepped in. He gazed in amazement: the path was overgrown with thistles and nettles; wild flowers and poppies were blooming in the garden. The trees were twisted. And the gardener stood by his side as the king gazed around. And he stopped and he listened. He heard the rustle of the little ones in the grasses, the squeak of the rabbit, the squeak and grunt of the hedgehog, the singing of the mistle thrush, the singing of the blackbird and the thrush – and they built their nests in the trees – the cry of the rook as it flew overhead. And a big smile crossed the king's face.

Turning to the gardener he said, "Thank you, gardener, now I have the most beautiful garden in the world, for my little ones have come back to me." And the king was happy with his garden.

THE TAILOR AND
THE BUTTON

I hope you're going to enjoy this story and that you'll remember it. I hope you'll tell it many years from now when I'm gone from this land.

A long time ago there once lived a little tailor. And this little tailor was very clever, for he was the cleverest tailor in all the land, and he worked for the king. Oh, he made beautiful dresses for the princesses and gowns and cloaks for the queen, and cloaks for the king. He worked so hard for the royal palace. The king was very proud of his little tailor. But because he worked so hard the little tailor never had time to make any clothes for himself. And soon his own clothes got worn and he was in rags.

One day, when he appeared before the king, the king said, "Tailor, how dare you come before me in such a state! You're in rags. You just look like a beggar man. Don't I pay you enough money to make some clothes for yourself?"

And the little tailor bowed before the king and said, "Yes, my sire, my lord, you pay me enough money. But you see I don't have time, because I also work for some people in the village and I make clothes for them."

"Well," the king said, "this will never do! You must never come before me in such a state again, because you put me to shame being my favourite tailor."

And then the king clapped his hands, called for the footman

to come before him. The footman came and bowed before the king.

The king said, "Footman, I want you to go down to the palace stores and bring me a roll of cloth." Cloth came in beautiful rolls and the king bought it this way.

So, the footman went off. In a few moments he returned with a beautiful roll of cloth, the nicest cloth in the whole palace. And the king caught it and held it between his hands.

"Now," he said, "tailor! Do you see this beautiful roll of cloth? I want you to take this home and make yourself a coat – the most beautiful coat you have ever made in your life. Now be gone with you, tailor, and never return before me till you make yourself the finest coat in all the land!"

Oh, the little tailor was happy. He carried the roll of cloth home with him, put it on his little bench. And he clipped and he stitched and he sewed all day long. He made the most beautiful coat that he had ever made in his life.

When he wore it to the village and when he wore it to the palace, people looked, they pointed and said, "Hey, look at the tailor! Look at the tailor's coat! Isn't that a beautiful coat the tailor has? Oh, I wish we had a coat like that!"

But no one had a coat like the tailor. And when he appeared before the king, the king was overjoyed, and the tailor was happy. For he had the most beautiful coat in all the land! The tailor wore his coat, he wore it and wore and wore it, and soon it was all worn through.

And then the little tailor brought his coat home and he said, "I can still do something with this." So, he spread the coat on his little bench and he clipped and he stitched and he sewed. From the coat he made a jacket – the most beautiful jacket you ever saw in your life.

And when he walked to the village, people looked, they pointed and said, "Hey, look at the tailor! Look at that jacket the tailor's wearing! Isn't that the most beautiful jacket we've ever seen in wir life? Oh, I wish we had a jacket like that."

But no one had a jacket like the tailor. And when he appeared before the king, the king was overjoyed to see the tailor in such a beautiful jacket. The little tailor was happy. He wore his jacket and he wore it and wore it, and soon his jacket was all worn through.

But the little tailor took the jacket home and spread it on his bench, and he said, "I can still do something with this."

So, he took his scissors and he clipped and he stitched and he sewed all day long. And from the jacket he made a waistcoat – the most beautiful waistcoat you ever saw in all your life!

When he wore it to the village, people looked and they pointed and said, "Hey, hey, look at the tailor! Look at that waistcoat the tailor's wearing! Isn't that the most beautiful waistcoat we have ever seen in our life? Oh, I wish we had a waistcoat like that."

But no one had a waistcoat like the tailor. And when he appeared before the king, the king was overjoyed to see the tailor in such a beautiful waistcoat. The little tailor was happy. And he wore his waistcoat, he wore it and he wore it and soon his little waistcoat was all worn through.

So, the little tailor took the waistcoat home, he spread it on his bench and said, "I can still do something with this." He took his scissors and he clipped, he stitched and he sewed all day long. From the waistcoat he made a beautiful little cap – the most beautiful little cap you ever saw in your life!

And when he wore it to the village, people looked and they pointed, they said, "Hey, hey, look at the tailor! Look at that cap the tailor's wearing! Wouldn't it be nice if we had a cap like that?"

Everyone wanted a cap like the tailor but no one could have a cap like the tailor. Because the cap the tailor had made was special for himself.

When he appeared before the king, the king was overjoyed to see the tailor in such a beautiful cap. And the little tailor was happy. He wore his little cap, he wore it and wore it to the envy of everybody, and soon it was all worn through.

And then the little tailor took his little cap home, he put it on the bench and said, "I can still do something with this." So, he took his scissors and he clipped, he stitched, he clipped and he stitched. From the cap he made a little bow tie – the most beautiful little bow tie you ever saw in all your life!

When he walked to the village, people looked and they pointed, they said, "Hey, look at the tailor! Look at that tie the tailor's wearing! Isn't that the most beautiful tie we have ever seen in wir life? Oh, I wish we had one like that. I wish we had a tie like the tailor." But no one had a tie like the tailor.

When he wore it before the king, the king was very pleased to see the tailor in his beautiful tie. And the little tailor was happy. He wore it and wore it to the envy of everybody, and soon the little tailor's tie was all worn through.

He took the little tie home and put it on his bench, he said, "I can still do something with this."

So, he took his scissors, he clipped and stitched and he clipped and stitched, and from the tie he made a little cloth button. Because cloth buttons were very popular in these days gone by.

And when he wore his little button to the village, people looked and pointed, they said, "Hey… hey, look at that button the tailor's wearing! Isn't that the most beautiful button we've ever seen? Oh, I wish we had a button like that, I wish we had fifty like that!" But no one had a button like the tailor.

And when the king spied the button he was very impressed by the tailor's button. The little tailor was very happy. And the tailor wore his little button, he wore it and wore it and soon his little button was all worn through.

The little tailor took his button home, even though he felt sad at heart, and he put his little button on the bench. And he said to himself, "I can still do something with this…"

And from his little button he made a story. And that's the story I have told to you just now!

GLOSSARY OF SCOTTISH WORDS

The Travelling People of Scotland have their own way of speaking. They use many Scottish forms of English words, such as *o'* (of), *canna* or *cannae* (cannot), *no* (not) and *tellt* (told). In their speech the word "of" is often left out when they refer to quantity or amount: *plenty* (plenty of) and *wee drop* (small amount of). Sometimes the storyteller's choice of words is influenced by the Gaelic language; for example, "was just after bringing" (had just brought) is found in the Western Highlands, where Duncan Williamson grew up. Readers will clearly understand most words and phrases in the context of the stories, but those terms more foreign to English are shown below:

alow:	below
bairn:	child
ben:	towards the inner room
bit:	bit of a (the)
but:	and
burkit:	kidnapped by body-snatchers
by:	in comparison with
ceilidh:	visit for storytelling and singing
coup:	tip out, empty
cowple:	fall over, collapse
crack:	small talk, news, converse
dinna(e):	do not
doubt:	expect

dram:	small drink of whisky
feart:	afraid
forbyes:	as well as, besides
greet:	cry, weep
heck:	rack in a stable for animal feed
henwife:	old woman who stayed on her own and kept hens and ducks, said to have special powers
ken(t):	know (knew)
laird:	landowner
landed:	arrived
lug:	ear
many's a year:	a long time
ower:	over
naebody:	anybody
oxter:	underarm, armpit
permanty:	bag, money sack
plooks:	pimples
puckle:	small amount (of)
raiked:	searched thoroughly through
set sail:	started on a journey
tattery:	ragged
tottery:	messy
thae:	that
theirself:	himself, herself
two-three:	a few
universt:	turned into one
weans:	children
wir:	our
wonst:	once
ye, ye're:	you, you're

The Shifty Lad
AND THE TALES HE TOLD

Peter Snow

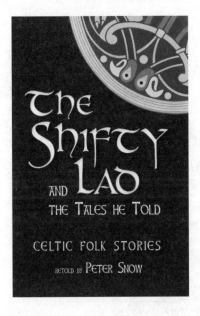

A wonderful collection of tales from Ireland, Wales and Scotland as told by the Shifty Lad who is using his storytelling gift to escape a terrible fate.

www.florisbooks.co.uk

SECRETS, ADVENTURES AND DANGER
WITH THE KELPIES CLASSICS

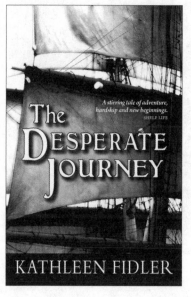

Twins Kirsty and David Murray are forced to leave their crofting home in the north of Scotland, and struggle to cope with life in Glasgow, where the work is hard and dangerous. Then comes a chance for a new adventure on a ship bound for Canada.

Will they survive the treacherous Atlantic crossing, and what will they find in the strange new land?

www.florisbooks.co.uk

Kali and Brockan are in trouble. They have been using their stone axes to chip limpets off the rocks, but they've gone too far out and find themselves trapped by the tides. Then, an unexpected rescuer appears, a strange boy in a strange boat, carrying a strangely sharp axe of a type they have never seen before.

Conflict arises as the village of Skara must decide what to do with the new ideas and practices that the boy brings. As a deadly storm threatens, the very survival of the village is in doubt.

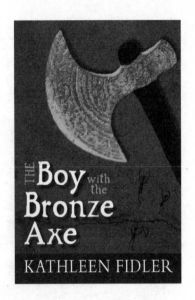

When Finn Learson staggers out of a stormy sea into a village on the Shetland Isles, he brings a secret with him. While the other villagers are enchanted by the stranger, Robbie suspects he's hiding something. Haunted by tales of the Selkie Folk, Robbie sees clues everywhere – the strange coin, the missing ship, Finn's love for Robbie's sister and her golden hair. But can Robbie convince the others in time to save his sister?

www.florisbooks.co.uk

The King of Ireland's Son
An Irish Folk Tale
Padraic Colum

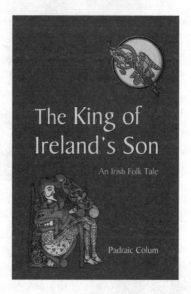

The King of Ireland's Son sets out to find the Enchanter of the Black Back-Lands and meets the Enchanter's daughter, Fedelma. His adventures lead him to the Land of the Mist, the Town of the Red Castle, and the worlds of Gilly of the Goatskin, Princess Flame-of-Wine, and the Giant Crom Duv.

This is a true Irish wonder tale: a coming of age story of the youngest son of the King of Ireland who sets off on an impossible quest. The stories weave together, stories within stories, in a fantastic tapestry of humour, poetry, action and adventure. Perfect for reading aloud at bedtime, generations of children have loved Padraic Colum's unmatched storytelling.

www.florisbooks.co.uk